TELLERS
OF
TALES

An anthology of verse and prose
by Soroptimists worldwide

Compiled by members of
Soroptimist International of Canterbury

Tellers of Tales
first published August 2013
by Soroptimist International (Canterbury)

EDITOR: Jacque Emery
DESIGN: Rachel Manby
COVER PICTURE: 'The Three Graces' by Liz West

For more information visit the Soroptimist UK website:
soroptimist-gbi.co.uk

World Literature Anthology

BIC: DCQ
ISBN 978-0-9926171-0-3

Printed and bound in Great Britain by
CPI Anthony Rowe, Chippenham, Wiltshire

FOREWORD

It is a pleasure to contribute a few words in a foreword to this wonderful collection. Here, you will find stories and poems which will make you laugh, cry and think. They are written by women from many continents, from Dundee to Durban, and from all four Soroptimist Federations. The writings embody all that is best about Soroptimist International: women from around the world coming together to use their creative skills and rich cultural diversity as a global voice for their sisters. That voice is truly needed when we consider that a woman dies in childbirth every minute of every day and in Sub-Saharan Africa a woman is 75% more likely to die in childbirth than in the developed world.

Many thanks to all who have contributed to writing and producing this book and to you for helping the BIG Project by buying it. I hope that you really enjoy reading *Tellers of Tales* and that you will continue your support for our global movement to inspire action and transform the lives of women and girls.

Margaret Oldroyd
July 2013

President Elect
Soroptimist International Great Britain and Ireland (SIGBI) Ltd

Margaret Oldroyd became a Soroptimist in 1986. She was attracted by the international character of the organisation and the opportunity to work with like-minded women to improve the lives of women and girls worldwide. Margaret is currently President Elect of Soroptimist International Great Britain and Ireland which includes 29 countries. She spent three very enjoyable years on the UK Programme Action Committee, has served as Club and Region President and been a Federation Councillor representing members in the Midlands. She has been involved in the organisation of both Federation and International conferences and has served on the Federation Management Board as Director of Organisational Development. But first and foremost she is a member of Soroptimist International of Nottingham which she thinks is the best club in the world! Margaret is a chartered librarian and has worked in colleges and universities delivering information skills courses and providing learning resources services. In the second part of her career, she was involved exclusively in staff management and development and quality enhancement projects. She held a number of posts in her professional association, the Chartered Institute of Library and Information Professionals, of which she is a Fellow and was particularly involved in the assessment of both professional and para-professional qualifications. She is now a magistrate on the Nottingham Bench and finds the work both challenging and rewarding. Margaret has a lifelong love affair with the theatre and is an avid reader. She is an active supporter of ActionAid, Book Aid International and the Africat Foundation (Namibia). She is a member of Nottinghamshire County Cricket Club and an Associate Member of the Royal Shakespeare Company. She likes watching cricket, travel, visiting gardens, gardening and bird-watching. Last, but definitely not least, she loves cats – large and small.

CONTENTS

TALES OF TRAVEL

TALES OF LIFE

TALES OF SOROPTIMISM

JUST TALES

INTRODUCTION

After the success of *Voices in Verse*, a book of poetry written by Soroptimists from all over the world, the members of one club, Canterbury, in the South East of England, invite you to join them in reading their second collection, *Tellers of Tales*.

From the beginning of time, 'tales' have been told in rhyme or verse form, others in prose. These stories about life, gods, goddesses, heroes, heroines and cultural traditions were often just spoken because their inspiration was fanned by the flames of camp fires and they originated long before the storytellers were able to put pen to paper.

This book presents 76 original 'tales' in both verse and prose, written by 48 writers from 14 countries. The 'tellers' share a common bond in being members of Soroptimist International, a women's organisation committed to 'making a difference' in the lives of others. The 'tales' are to be shared over a cup of coffee, pot of tea or glass of wine.

They include reminiscences of childhood, memories of journeys, lifetime experiences, Soroptimist activities or 'just tales'. We laugh and cry with the writers as we picture the soggy, knitted bathing costume at an English seaside resort in the 1960s, read about escaping from an earthquake in New Zealand, being mistaken for a ghost in Yorkshire or staying at a hotel of dubious reputation in Macau!

We invite you to celebrate the power, passion and humour of the written word as you accompany us on our journey with the *Tellers of Tales*.

Tellers of Tales

There are tales to be told
In the streets of New York,
In the diners of Denver,
The boulevards of Paris.

There are tales to be told
Under swaying palms,
In a grandmother's arms,
Sharing rice and ackee.

There are tales to be told
Through memories' mists,
Of an age long ago,
In a world long-forgotten.

There are tales to be told
And lifetimes to share,
To preserve and pass on
To an age yet to come.

There are tales
                    to be told.

Jacque Emery (SI Canterbury, England)

TALES OF CHILDHOOD

Carol Salter *lives in Manston, East Kent, England and has been a Soroptimist for six years. She is currently Vice President of SI Canterbury. Carol has been a nurse for many years and has worked in a variety of settings, including being a plaster/ minor operations nurse and a charge nurse in a drug team. In more recent years she has worked as a health visitor and school nurse. She is also a prolific writer and runs writers' workshops. She loves reading, writing, cats and food – but not necessarily in that order! She has been married for 22 years and has a 13 year old son.*

The Mother I Don't Know and My Selfish Ways

My mother doesn't speak about her childhood but I know it wasn't good from the lack of information she imparts. Today she says, "Don't ask me. I can't remember those days any more," but I think she can. She goes out of her way to avoid being alone. At 81 plus she walks round the nearby town every day. She travels with her walker, negotiating buses, going to lunch clubs, evening bingo and social events at local working men's clubs – places where I grew up.

My mother used to knit and sew – a lot. She worked, when I was very young, for a designer clothes factory 'Martonys'. She was proud of her work. She had friends and a position. When it closed down in the early 1960s she took cleaning jobs at nearby shops to help bring in money and make ends meet.

My dad was a gas lamp lighter. He lit the old town lamps at night and turned them off come morning, then he'd toil from dawn to dusk as a hod carrier until his retirement. I didn't know him well. I knew the bullet wound scars in his calves, the shrapnel in his back from WWII, his short temper, his love of beer and cats.

As a child I didn't realise my mum was illiterate. I knew she had missed a lot of schooling. From what she doesn't say her mother was depressed and unhappy. Mum listened when I was seven reading my 'Janet & John' books to her. I expected her to correct me if I was wrong but she never did – never could. I never knew.

She was good at repairs and alterations though. Our home was full to bursting with trousers, curtains and shirts piled high in her kitchen. It made a fair addition to the home income but we went without some nights. The stockpot lasted for months on the hob in winter, mostly vegetables but sometimes a sliver of meat. Soup and dumplings on the lean days and mashed potato with leftovers or tinned sardines. We looked at the fruit bowl. It was for guests not us, haliborange was the closest we came to fruit.

I guess I was an ungrateful child and most of all when it came to clothes. My mum made many of them. I hated them. I hated the pity and scorn from school acquaintances, never friends, at my pathetic state of dress. Knitted socks and vests when I was ten, the embarrassment, the shame. Knitted swimming costumes which left the beach three minutes after me complete with mini rock pool and shrimp catch of the day. White bottom crease exposed to the sun, bathers and their children pointing and laughing.

At repairs and alterations my mum excelled. From taking up or in, trousers, skirts and dresses to huge velvet curtain repairs. But designing, or creating from scratch? Not so great and not in time. Sleeves patched, or worse removed and replaced with 'good enough' sleeves from other shirts. As young teenagers we'd share our fashion plans, the culotte fabric sat in the repair pile years after the style had gone and I'd outgrown them.

Worst of all, my school uniform. "Not buying those, too expensive" she'd cry. Skirts made of crimplene, caught on every splinter of wood on every desk in school until they resembled strings of thread spaghetti. Jumpers made from a continuous roll of tube sweater material she got 'cheap'. Cut two holes for sleeves; attach another piece in the hole and 'tada'! One school jumper – not.

My mum went on to sew until two years ago. In that time she must have repaired thousands of clothes. She did make clothes that were fine for me. It's funny how I remember the hideous outfits and have to think hard to recall the brilliant Bay City Roller outfit, the flared trousers, the engagement dress and my favourite, the fur she added to my winter coats, fur from jumble sale offerings which made me look like a princess. Not to mention the ballroom dress when I was six.

I try to consider what lessons I've learnt. Because be sure every task, every act or omission has a lesson to give. I guess the two most valuable to me, are how to cope with ridicule and embarrassment but more importantly, that every stitch my mother sewed was placed there with love for me.

Carol Salter (SI Canterbury, England)

Marie Blacktop *was born in Blackburn, England and has lived in the Ribble Valley in Lancashire for 38 years. She was a teacher for 33 years, and latterly Deputy Head of a comprehensive school until she took early retirement. Since then she has been a volunteer at a local primary school helping with their reading partnership scheme. Marie is married to Roy and they celebrated their Ruby Wedding in July 2009. They have two children and two grandchildren. Marie joined Blackburn Soroptimists 16 years ago and has been Club President, Regional Press and Publicity Officer, Regional Vice-President and Regional President Elect. She was Regional President for North West England and the Isle of Man in 2009. Apart from Soroptimism, Marie enjoys walking, theatre, reading and travel and she is a season ticket holder and life-long supporter of Blackburn Rovers football club.*

The Paddling Pool

It was back in the days when children roamed free,
Roller-skating, running, climbing a tree.
With friends I was allowed to go to the park,
Just feeding the ducks and having a lark.

The best place of all was the paddling pool;
We loved splashing around and playing the fool,
But disaster struck when I climbed out at last.
I'd trodden on a shard of broken glass.

My friend who lived nearest ran home to her mum
Who, rather reluctantly, decided to come.
She obviously thought I was making a fuss
And duly dispatched me back home on the bus.

The conductor was kinder and let me on free
And happily my mother did not chastise me.
She called out our doctor who pulled out the glass
And told me he thought I was a brave little lass.

Next day I should have been back in my class,
But luckily for me this did not come to pass.
An elderly neighbour, now wheel-chair bound,
Had seen all the commotion and had pushed herself round.

She offered to lend me her own special chair,
So I couldn't complain that life was not fair.
I was not stuck at home, indoors and downbeat,
But could whiz up and down quite fast in the street.

So a trip to the park was really quite tame
And that paddling pool was never the same!

Marie Blacktop (SI Blackburn, England)

Lexi Smart *was born in the Vale of Strathmore, Angus in North East Scotland within a few miles of Glamis Castle, the childhood home of HM the Queen Mother and the birthplace of Princess Margaret. The Castle is also the legendary setting of Shakespeare's play Macbeth and has a ghost called the Green Lady! Lexi was educated at Websters Seminary, Kirriemuir – the birthplace of the famous playwright JM Barrie, creator of Peter Pan. She had a long career within the private and public sectors working in human resource management development. A Soroptimist since 1999, Lexi is currently Programme Action Officer in the Dundee Club; she has been Club President twice in 2004-05 and 2010-11 and Region President, Scotland North in 2009-10. Lexi is married to Stewart. She enjoys travel, photography and classical music, especially at the annual evening event of 'Proms in the Park' at Glamis Castle.*

Snow Time in Scotland

Winter time is well upon us by December, January and February each year, often going on into April when we have a spell of very cold temperatures and sometimes milder weather throughout the UK. With Scotland being furthest north it is easily assumed we have loads upon loads of snow all the time! Imagine if we did, we then could have masses of snowmen appearing in all the gardens and parks!! One of my great passions is snowmen (and women) of course, so I wish it was true!

Santa has real competition when I buy our Christmas decorations each year – the snowmen win hands down every time. I have smiley faced snowmen in every shape and size imaginable and annually add to my collection! Each year we bring them down from the attic with the Christmas tree and tinsel. They arrive like little visitors we all enjoy for a few weeks – until they go back up for next year. One little beige coloured snowman with a brown hat and orange carrot nose escaped the packing box one year and did not go back to the attic! He enjoyed being out all year long – but of course we had to tell everyone that he was really Mr Parsnip not a snowman out of season – he was so embarrassed!

My earliest memory of snow falls was as a child in the 1940s (Ssh!) a four year old girl – all agog and scared witless with the thundering of the giant snow plough that passed our house every day until the snow started to disappear. I remember it also seemed to be driven by a very scary looking man. The depth of the snow was in feet rather than the few inches or centimetres we generally get nowadays. Helped by the fierce winds the snow was at least five to six feet deep which meant when walking any distance people were walking with a stick on top of the fences, walls and hedges rather than beside them! When we had gale force winds the snow would often reach the roofs of the houses!

Snow soon brings flooding, frost and ice. We spent many happy winters as children, skating on our homemade ice rink – just a flat flooded field frozen over and all with our school shoes on of course!! Oh! The raging from our Mums and Dads could be heard far into the distance!! *Dancing on Ice* would have had no look in with us – but there again there were no televisions in those bygone days – at least not in 'normal' houses like ours!!

As I write this article we have just had a very bad snow fall – but is it really bad? In modern day terms this five inches or so is a calamity according to our nation of pampered people and the media – but compared with way back in the 1940s and 50s this is tame stuff! We are not walking on fencing, walls or hedges as we did long ago – nowadays thankfully, we can leave that for the birds and squirrels!

Lexi Smart (SI Dundee, Scotland)

Clare Harding *was born in Louth, Lincolnshire, England, but now lives in Blackburn, Lancashire. She worked as a teacher for 12 years and then spent 21 years as a teacher and tutor for the National Childbirth Trust. She is now 'retired' but has a new career as a Desktop Publisher. She has one son, an ecologist, who lives in Scotland. Competing demands from her church during the vacancy of a priest have meant that she has had to reduce her commitment to SI Blackburn, but she still enjoys designing literature for their projects and events. Clare loves classical, especially religious music, walking, natural history and writing.*

School

At nearly-nine,
Corralled in a barred yard:
Brick walls and tar macadam,
We lined up in crocodiles,
Entering, at the barked order of a bell,
The vestibule, where thick slabs
Of bristling coir ambushed awkward,
Unwary ankles, and the surly caretaker
Leant on his long broom.
Forty-eight of us,
Iron-yoked in pairs,
(leaving a couple of desks for sinners);
The tip-up seat had an uncertain temper,
Administering a smart slap
To the back of the legs if provoked.
Rote, rule and ruler reigned,
The droning dame.

but dust danced dervishes in the searchlights
punched through quarantine rectangles of sky
which castellated the tall walls
which framed
        the brumous blink
of a single street-lamp
        presaging tea and toast in comfy winter homecomings,

corybantic cloud-charades,
black swift-scimitars slashing the solstice
   screaming blue fits of summer
         of Africa!

Clare Harding (SI Blackburn, England)

Eileen Clarke *was born in Kidderminster, Worcestershire, England. She was brought up and educated there and spent most of her adult life in that area. She went into the Worcestershire based family business at 18 which enabled her to spend much time engaged in voluntary work including the Samaritans, Parochial Church Council and Parish Council. She also helped set up an older peoples' network in Worcestershire with Worcestershire County Council. In 2005 Eileen moved to Lancashire, just after the birth of a much longed for first grandchild. She has also continued the voluntary work there and renewed her interest in Soroptimist International. She is married to Roland and they enjoy voluntary work together, gardening, reading, the countryside and discovering the joys of Lancashire with family and friends. They consider themselves to be very lucky. Eileen still keeps in touch with old school friends in Worcestershire.*

Looking Back with Affection
School Days 1945 (5 years) to 1956 (18 years)

Does memory play tricks – or so they say
How much was work? How much play?
When life was a dream the livelong day
And we shouted HOORAH and NEVER HOORAY!!

Once we were new and the prefects were OLD,
Incredibly grand, mature and bold.
'NO RUNNING IN CORRIDORS!' we were told
And no dodging showers, however cold!

Meekly in lessons we innocents sat,
Puzzling the meaning of words like 'begat'.
'I don't want to learn French!' one brave girl had said,
Taking the path no ANGELS dared tread.

As years passed our feelings were rather love/hate,
Strict rules and dictates a part of our fate
Ways that we had of not quite obeying,
Were many and varied – and more I'm not saying.

But the 13 years or so will stay with me forever
By what we achieved mediocre or clever
Many the friendships we would now never sever
Education for Life, 'Old Girls Forever.'

Eileen Clarke (SI Leyland, England)

Pansy Lineth Griffith *lives in the West Indies. She was born on the island of Grenada but now lives in Barbados. She is a parent and has two sons. Pansy has now retired after 35 years, but worked as a specialist in early childhood education. She taught Reception and Kindergarten classes at St. Gabriel's Primary School and launched and operated 'Aunty Pansy's Day Care Centre'. Pansy loves flowers and is a member of the Barbados Flower Arranging Society. She was the President in 2000-03. She is also a member of the Barbados Horticultural Society, Barbados Association of Flower Arrangers, Grenada Association of Flower Arrangers and the World Association of Flower Arrangers. She is also a Cub Scouts Leader and a Family and Social Counsellor. Pansy is a committed Soroptimist and was President of SI Barbados – hosting the SIGBI conference in 2008. Pansy's hobbies include cooking, swimming, walking, singing, gardening, reading, travel and scrabble. She is a crossword puzzle enthusiast and loves opera and theatre.*

Errol and the Ghost

This story is true, true, true. I was there with my mischievous big brother and my bored younger sister.

The neighbours were kind, courteous and extremely careful not to upset anyone in the village since most of them were blood-related. My father was one such member, having many cousins – one of whom lived on my street. He was a smallish man of Indian descent, with a high-pitched voice and laughing eyes. He was a gardener by day and I guess a busy man in his spare time since his wife was now expecting their eleventh child. Errol was the ninth of the brood, still toddling and the favourite, since he was quite precocious – stringing words together, running simple errands, helping with the baby and winning everyone's affection.

My family was very well respected in the village. My father answered to the name 'cuz' as both young and old alike claimed him for their cousin. My mother was puritanical and we were taught to return the kindness and courtesy extended to us – but we were also expected to be good examples to those who did not attend Sunday school like we did. I was the middle of five children with a brother at each end. The big one was dependable and sometimes protective towards his siblings but he was very prankish and would find fun in quite mundane episodes. His imagination was fertile and one just never knew what was coming next.

As Errol's family members took their rightful places in the world, having grown up, he decided to remain at his mother's side. His father was now crippled from arthritis and his mother depended on his strength and fortitude. He was fearless and well respected by all who knew him, especially his peers in the village and wider environs. He was part of whatever was happening – so much so that whenever anyone needed information about anything, Errol was consulted and his opinion revered. It was a case of the one-eyed man being a king in the blind kingdom!

During those care-free, stress-free days, the contented country folk travelled on foot and many walked long distances to reach their destinations. The church, the doctor, the dentist, the midwife, the school, the cinema and all the other important amenities were situated in the country town. Those who lived in the remote areas within a ten mile radius had no choice but to walk. The few well-to-do families who owned any form of transportation like a horse or a donkey cart used it to their own advantage. The others executed their business by setting off very early in the morning and getting home by evening.

Well, Errol ran errands for many and he travelled well within daylight hours. However, as he became part of the environment, his amorous escapades got the better of him and he slowly but surely became a 'midnight marauder' much to the displeasure of his kith and kin. They reminded him of the evil spirits which roamed the deserted areas after midnight. They warned him of the beautiful woman in white who has one real foot and one cow's hoof and whose sweet smile enchants into oblivion. They spoke in hushed tones about the big black and white dog which followed Mr. Moombay when he went for the midwife on Good Friday night and the child was born dead the next morning. They begged and pleaded with him to avoid walking through the village cemetery by himself after 10pm because the ghosts were out at that time to see who they could find to trip-up and suck their blood after they lost consciousness. They assured him that our street was safe but he should not push his luck since some of our departed foreparents are buried between our house and his house.

My mother was getting old and restless at the time and her erratic cat-naps were disturbed most nights by Errol's heavy footsteps along the track and his whistling or humming to himself which woke the dog and started him barking. My big brother was not amused by this and he asked Errol to reconsider his hours. He was told that duty and business kept him out later than he had bargained for but he would try.

The weeks went by and there were no changes. My brother decided that he would take matters in hand. My younger sister was home on vacation and was bored to tears. She offered to assist him with the matter. I got scared not knowing what they were but decided to look from a distance. That night, as luck would have it, Errol did not stay out because an old lady who was ailing for a long time had died and he was asked to accompany his mother to the wake. This gave my impish brother sufficient time to plan his strategy with the sister who was now wide awake and full of unrighteous energy.

Well, the wheels of invention began grinding as soon as Errol made his way from home that evening. My brother and sister went to the back of our house where the family cemetery was located. This also happened to be Errol's pathway to his house. They collected some 'things' with which they built a large scarecrow. Then they dressed it with a white sheet, placed a kind of hat on the head, put the arms outstretched as if to enfold someone and leaned it to a position as if taking a forward step. They then sprinkled some white flour on the dark pathway and doused the whole area with a concoction of white rum, perfume, petrol and coke to which copious amounts of black pepper powder was added. They themselves began to sneeze uncontrollably! After they had completed their mischief, they looked at it and were scared out of their wits. They quickly hurried back to the house, turned off all the lights, gave my mother a sedative and settled down for the onslaught.

It was not too long before the thump, thump, thump, of Errol's boots were heard pounding down the pathway. Then suddenly, a scream, a shriek, a yell, a bellow, a howl, as a breathless Errol was concording back up the pathway bawling for mercy as the dog was pursuing him with a vengeance! We waited until his voice was inaudible, then we quickly retrieved the 'spectre' which, I must admit, was terrifyingly frightening. We removed all the physical evidence but deliberately left the flour and the evil-smelling concoction so that when he told his story to everyone who would listen that day, they could not doubt him. Some of them said "I told you so". Others shuddered. Still some others said it was the ghost of the dead old lady who had come for him. In all of this, they never stopped sneezing when they came to view the place where the ghost had appeared and as for Errol the Intrepid? He never walked that way again.

My mother was able to sleep peacefully, my brother never spoke a word of it without collapsing with laughter and my sister quickly learnt the tricks of the trade. I saw it all and still could not believe what my brother had done!

Pansy Griffith (SI Barbados)

Sheilah Downs *was born in Barnet, Hertfordshire, England. During the latter years of WWII she was evacuated to Durham City until the war ended. Prior to emigration to New Zealand in 1964 with her family, Sheilah worked as a nurse in Yorkshire and in Watford, then later as a Secretary with Pirelli in London. Once in New Zealand she continued with her career in the commercial world, holding positions as Personnel Manager with Phillips Electrical and other electronic manufacturing companies. Sheilah has been a member of her local Lower Hutt Soroptimist club since 1972, having filled all the various executive roles, including twice as President. She has also held the position of National President and President of the Central Region of New Zealand. She has been honoured to receive Honorary Life Membership of both her club and the Central Region. In her spare time Sheilah is also organiser and founder of a local branch of the Evacuees' Reunion Association and, together with two other branch members, was elected National Secretary last year. 'Keep Calm and Carry On' is always kept in mind!*

Evacuation

As a child in Britain during WWII, I was evacuated together with my mother and baby sister. We went from Barnet in North London to the city of Durham. There I went to a school which I think must have been a church school as it was reached by walking through the cemetery. We sat on bench seats with a writing ledge built into them. The classroom had only high windows which meant there were no outside distractions!

Outside I remember a grassed area where we played at break times and which had a goat tethered there. I remember my mother being very upset when I had to report that the goat had eaten my hair ribbons due to my curiosity and getting too close to him.

At the end of the street where I was living was a large bombed site. This was all fenced off with 'Keep Out' notices, however I seem to remember that was one of our favourite play areas – that is until I fell off a wall into some barbed wire and had to go home with a bleeding face and admit where I had been!

An experience occurred on the way home from school one afternoon. My friends (mostly boys I seem to remember) were idly collecting dead leaves from the footpath which we used to break up and stuff into small clay pipes to smoke!!

All of a sudden this plane appeared above us and started machine gunning us as we ran down the road. We hurled ourselves over someone's garden wall and crouched down until the plane had disappeared, then eagerly ran out to collect the bullets from the road to be shown as souvenirs of our exciting escape from death!

This was just another example of what must have been a fairly frequent event as the planes came over regularly on bombing raids to the Tyneside shipyards in nearby Newcastle. Once they had made their run they circled south over Durham on their way back to bases on the continent – anything left over by way of bombs or bullets were used as they flew over Durham.

Sheilah Downs (SI Lower Hutt, New Zealand)

Joan Lees *is an ex-teacher who has written since childhood. She lives in Stoke, Nelson, New Zealand. She is a charter member of Soroptimist International of Waimea, in Richmond, Nelson, New Zealand. It was formed in 1974 and belongs to the Region of New Zealand South and the Federation of the South-West Pacific. Joan has been Club President and she has attended various conferences as a club delegate. Her other interests are Girl Guiding, church, family and Scottish country dancing. Joan enjoys taking part in poetry readings.*

On 3 February 1931, most of Napier was levelled by an earthquake. 256 people were killed by the ensuing fires and collapse of buildings. Thousands more were injured. The coastline was altered forever when over 40 kilometres of the sea bed surfaced and became dry land.

Napier, 3 February 1931

I held my brother's hand
as we walked the few blocks to school.
He was my big brother – all of six years old.
He wore a blue shirt and navy trousers;
I wore a cream tussore dress and navy tie.
School was still new and strange,
reading, sums and handwriting all mysteries.

The bell rang, and we were finally free
for a brief time, before playtime ended,
and we, like wild things, were caged again,
release an age away at three.
Suddenly, a rumbling roar
filled our morning, shook our world.
We cowered and cried, only partly soothed
by the teacher's trembling voice
as she marshalled us outside
and we were sent home.

A naval ship radios the news:
Hundreds of miles to the north
Napier lies in ruins and burning.
Children like us die in collapsed schools.
Islands and rocks rise from the sea.

Joan Lees (SI Waimea, New Zealand)

Lieske Bester *was born in Malang, Indonesia and has been proudly South African since 1963. She was educated in Java in a WWII concentration camp and then in the Netherlands. She was an officer in the W.R.Neth.N.S from 1951-57 and married a South African Naval officer in 1957. Lieske has three daughters and four grandchildren. She worked as a Director of a Drama/Life Skills Workshop for 21 years and is still active as a theatre reviewer, adjudicator and facilitator. Lieske was a founder member of SI False Bay and was President twice. She was Secretary of Soroptimist International of South Africa (SISA) from 1991-93. She transferred to SI Cape of Good Hope in 1994 and was Club Secretary from 2009-11. Lieske's hobbies are travel, all aspects of theatre, reading and re-cycling. Her project passions are the Club stall at Community Chest Carnival and Lourier Primary School Library. She speaks English, Afrikaans, Dutch, German and rusty French (which improves with a good cognac). Lieske is not domestically accomplished or inclined! She loves dogs, dolphins and sunflowers.*

Memories of Once Upon a Time

I was born in Malang, Java and amongst the many fond memories of life in the Dutch East Indies (now Indonesia) before WWII are the indigenous festivals that my young brother and I were allowed to share. This included a sleep over at a reed home in the Kampong not far away from where we lived. Kokkie (our cook) ruled the domestic roost in our home (my mother was rarely allowed in her kitchen) and on a number of occasions gave Dick and me a real treat by inviting us to a celebration in her village.

We loved the familiar spicy and sweet snacks and the rose syrup and coconut milk drink and could have as much as we (literally) could stomach. When we were filled to the brim we joined the rest of the locals in the special space that was cleared for the evening's entertainment. This could be an elaborately costumed acting out of a historical or mythical event or a wajang (shadow puppet) show with similar themes, with or without narration.

It was the first theatrical experience of many in my life and I vividly remember the flames of the fires that lit up the stories of historical and mythical battles between heroes, heroines and villains, with the gamelans (drums and other percussion instruments) providing a magical sound track. The audience was equally fascinating – passionately involved and entranced as we were in spite or perhaps because of the familiarity of the tales. Looking back, I'd like to think that it was the beginning of the dramatic road I took later on as an actress, director and teacher!

My little brother sometimes fell asleep and at the end of the evening would be carried to our sleeping place – shared with Kokkie – each with our own mat on the earthen floor.

Magic memories of once upon a time…

Lieske Bester (SI Cape of Good Hope, South Africa)

Erene Grieve *has been a member of SI Milford Haven in Pembrokeshire, Wales, for 18 years. Having left school at 15 she went to University as a mature student. She started teaching in secondary school when she was 40 and after that worked for the Open University as a lecturer in Developmental Psychology. Now retired from paid employment she operates the 'Stamps in Schools' project which introduces children to the joys of stamp collecting. Sponsored by the British Postal Museum and Archive she travels throughout the UK and often meets Soroptimists on her travels. On one of her trips to Greece she was delighted to meet with local Soroptimists there. In her spare time she enjoys family history, philately, cycling, walking, writing, helping at the local theatre and learning Greek.*

What's in a Name?

I want you to consider that well-worn phrase 'what's in a name?' and I want to tell you what I think. Your name says who you are; it gives you an identity, a sense of belonging to a group – a family. It gives you a sense of place – where you come from; it gives you a history, a past and a future. You are your name and your name is you.

You might wonder why I am telling you all this. I want you to understand how I felt when I was told that the name I had been living with, the name by which I had identified myself, was actually not my name at all. Certainly there was a piece of paper, a birth certificate, that stated my name, but everything else that goes with having a name was closed to me.

I can't remember when my father first told me that he had changed his name from the one he was born with to one that he had plucked out of the air as a young man. What I can remember is the effect it had on me.

I am nine years old and it's lunch hour at Alexandra Park Primary School. I have a secret to tell and I am looking for my friends to share it with. My name isn't really Rene Hulton; my name is Erene Zlatano. I come from a family that lives in Greece and my Dad has changed his name. My friends are impressed.

But my glory is short-lived. Word spreads and as I cross the playground the taunts start. "You're a sultana! Sultana! Sulta-a-a-na!" Their faces are ugly with accusation, contorted by scorn. I want to take my secret back. In a flash of inspiration I point to my friends and shout "I fooled you! I was only joking. It wasn't true." My friends are stunned and I can feel their hostility. For a moment I have no friends and no glory either. The matter is never mentioned again, by them or by me.

I am 12 years old at grammar school collecting my homework from Mrs Thomas our English teacher. She calls me to the front. "And what is this," she barks at me peering down from her tall stool. "Why have you put Erene Zlatano E-r-e-n-e Z-l-a-t-a-n-o on your homework? Don't you know who you are?" she demands. I open my mouth to explain, but I am ordered back to my seat. I can feel the colour rush to my face.

Last night Grandad Z told me about Greece. He speaks Greek to me – it sounds wonderful. One day I will learn how to speak Greek too.

I am 14 years old. Today we have a new Latin teacher, Miss Collinwood. She tries to remember our names by reading them from the register and looking at our faces. And then she comes to me. Erene has never sounded more wonderful. "That's a Greek name," she says softly, surprised but smiling. "It's a lovely name, it means peace. I studied Greek at University." One day I'll go to University and I will learn Greek too.

I am 60, retired, and learning to use a computer. Today I will try using Google. Let's try Z-l-a-t-a-n-o. With a click of the mouse I meet my ancestors, the family I never knew.

I am 64 and at Gatwick Airport, waiting for the flight to Corfu and clutching my Greek phrase book. Today I will meet the family and I will be one of them – a Zlatano. And when I return home I will turn on my computer and with a click I will be on 'Ancestry' and there will be my name for all to see: 'Welcome Erene Zlatano'. And it will feel wonderful.

So you see there is something in a name, just as I told you. It's been a long journey, but no-one can say to me now "Don't you know who you are?"

Erene Grieve (SI Milford Haven, Wales)

Brenda Lynton-Escreet *has been a member of SI Morecambe and Heysham
for 15 years. She was born in Morecambe in Lancashire, North West England.
Adopted as a baby, she grew up in Kirby Lonsdale and Lancaster. She now
lives with her husband Malcolm, an engineer, in a tiny village on the edge of
Morecambe Bay. They have two daughters, two sons, four granddaughters and
three grandsons. They share their lives with two feisty rescue Italian greyhounds
and one splendid rescue cat. Brenda worked for Lancashire Youth and
Community Service for 28 years and following two working visits to Swaziland in
the 1990s, she founded Partners in Education Swaziland, a registered charity of
which she is now Patron. Brenda has secondary progressive Multiple Sclerosis and
is a disability activist. Committed to the promotion of equality for women and the
girl child she uses her writing to involve other people in the inclusion of Disabled
People in World Events and decision making. Her short story will be familiar to
Soroptimists everywhere and her poem was written in response to the birth of
her friend's daughter who has an extra chromosome. This wonderful girl child is
now in mainstream education (with appropriate support). Shame on anyone who
regards her as unfinished and refuses to recognise the joy she has brought to her
family and friends.*

Amniocentesis

Cradled in my silver throne
High on top of the shopping kart
I watch the motes of dust caught in the sunbeams
that pour in through the dusty windows

I play with my perfect pink toes
And remember the tides and watery shores of my mother's womb
I become aware of your approach

"Is it a girl?" You peer at me,
Recoil, with words of commiseration
Barely disguised revulsion
At the work of the extra chromosome
That has gently smudged my features.

Be careful of that cuckoo-like urge to push me out of the nest forever
For behind my unfocussed blue eyes
I hold the secret of your survival

Blessed Be

Brenda Lynton-Escreet (SI Morecambe and Heysham, England)

Nisha Ghosh *lives in Pune, India. She describes herself as a Soroptimist '100 percent of the time'. She is a freelance journalist and writer of all sorts. She is also a documentary film maker and teaches English to foreign students and high school children. For the rest of the time she likes to embroider mostly cross-stitch and read 'serious stuff'. Nisha has been a Soroptimist for the last 11 years. She has made documentary films of her club projects – one was showcased at the Montreal Convention in 2011 and the other at the Glasgow Convention in 2007. Nisha was the Founder President of SI Pune Metro East which she nurtured from its very beginning. She was the first Indian to be part of the Federation Team – as Friendship Link Coordinator for SIGBI. She is a single mother with a married son and a grandson.*

A Rare Life

One Friday afternoon in June 2004, I kissed her and tucked her to bed. She gave me her toothless smile and said, "Let me sleep." A couple of hours later when I went to wake her up, she had transited to another world. No doctors, no medicines, no hospitals – ever so peacefully. I was left with the memory of that last smile. Nafisa my precious first born had finished her time with me.

She had come to the world so quietly – no crying and fuss, just a little underweight baby I didn't know how to handle. But between these two serene moments there were 26 years of multiple problems. I was told that underweight babies pick up quickly, which never happened. She had delayed milestones which I was told didn't matter so much and that by the time she was six, she would catch up with other kids. It was only when she was three years old that I discovered through my readings that she may be a borderline case of Cerebral Palsy. The doctors then began to look at her differently. At least we knew on which path to tread. Later I took her to the Spastic Society in New Delhi and suddenly the darkness of not knowing was dispelled. I can't say that I wasn't haunted with the "why me?" question, but some inner strength took charge of the situation.

I learnt everything I could on the condition of Cerebral Palsy (CP). In Nafisa's case she was a spastic type. Unfortunately the causes of such disorders are still unknown. In my case I couldn't put my finger on any reason why Nafisa was born a CP child.

Acceptance on the part of the family is very important, for the child's rehabilitation progress and more for their own peace of mind. Yes it is tough, especially for the mother, but the rewards are there too. Imagine you are like the life line to your special child and the satisfaction of having done your best is immeasurable.

With Nafisa life was very different. Of course the pace of everything I did matched hers. There were a thousand things that I or her brother Anees couldn't do, but look at the sensitivity it gave us. That Anees became a sensitive human being, aware of others and their needs has something to do with the moments he had looking after his elder sister. She bullied him all right and he took it with dignity. She was Didi (elder sister) but often he had to even feed and carry her. With her sad eyes she often asked when she would grow up like her brother.

That never happened. Over the years she progressively lost her sight and then her hearing. By 18 she was completely blind. She had used a hearing aid since the age of eight but by her 23rd birthday it was no use and she was unable to hear at all. We adjusted our lives to suit hers but more than that she adjusted to each setback. By the age of 26 she had lost all her teeth and couldn't walk. What remained was her thick mop of curly hair, her fragile stature and her loving spirit. This sort of deterioration isn't normal with Cerebral Palsy.

Nafisa was a 'rare spastic'. Her name in Persian means rare and so she was in every way, until the very end when she gave me a rare smile and departed. I am consoled by everyone saying at least she is bereft of her deformed body and now her spirit flies free as it is meant to be. She has left us a legacy of wonderful memories and a receptivity that has enriched our lives.

Nisha Ghosh (SI Pune Metro East, India)

Hannah Mili Boteiova *was born and brought up in Suva, Fiji Islands, where she has lived for most of her working life. Hannah has had two careers – the first, as General Overseer of GWASUTH Ministry, and the second as a business entrepreneur and owner of her own business. Her ministerial work has given her many opportunities to travel around Fiji. Hannah became a Soroptimist and was made President-Elect of SI Suva in 2012. She enjoys reading, walking, and landscaping and plays darts for her club in Suva!*

Raised By Grannies

"Timaaaaaa! It's two o' clock. Put the kettle on! Prepare breakfast! Are there biscuits?"

"No grandpa, none. But I've already put the kettle on the stove and I'm going to collect firewood. I'll be back soon." Tima turned and disappeared into the nearby bush.

At 13, Tima lived with her grandparents, who were too old to earn any money for Tima's education. Tima did chores while the young boys (three of them) went to school. Tima's father left when she was six months old and before her first birthday, her mother left too to go and work. In spite of this the salary she sent home still wasn't sufficient to provide for the education of her children, with the exception of Tima's two older brothers. Her grandparents were too old to run around and Tima was perfect for the job since she was young and energetic. The only disadvantage was, because of this, Tima didn't have the slightest bit of scholarly knowledge. She didn't even know the alphabet! When she started fires with old newspapers, she would stare at the written material with a strange expression. While her brothers were doing their homework, Tima would sit behind them and peep over their shoulders in wonderment. The more she stared, the more intrigued she became.

Sometimes she'd lie in bed, wondering about her future. "Where will I be, what will I do? My grandparents won't be around forever. When they pass away, then what? Who will marry me? I can't work, because I can't fill in forms. Oh God, what will my future be?"

At 21, Tima still couldn't write her name. She wept remembering her grandmother's words. "Don't worry Tima, although you didn't attend school, you've developed skills that the most educated people would pay for – cooking, cleaning, washing, collecting sea products and taking care of others. I pray God will give you a loving husband, who'll understand you despite your illiteracy." Tima never forgot those meaningful words. "There'll be employers who will teach you. May God grant you all that, my girl."

When Tima was 25 years old her grandfather passed away – followed two years later by her grandmother. Such loneliness caused Tima to often become depressed. Eventually, she found work as a housemaid and was happy to be self-sufficient. Alas, her boss was sometimes cruel, but Tima never forgot her grandmother's words of God.

Not long after this, a young man of chiefly status was attracted to Tima and pursued her. He sent his servant to ask Tima's uncle for her hand in marriage. This was willingly given and Tima was married in a chiefly ceremony. She has been married now for the past 12 years and in all this time she has never suffered any form of physical or verbal abuse from her husband.

Two years ago Tima was interviewed by another boss and she now works in a house occupied by two ladies and their daughters. The two ladies are sisters who are very kind to her. The younger one has begun to teach Tima to read and write. Tima continues to progress in her learning, thanks to the sisters who currently employ her.

Hence, trust God. He orchestrates the best endings.

Hannah Mili Boteiova (SI Suva, Fiji)

Monica Barry *has been a very active member of SI Sligo for 30 years and held*
every office there at one time or another. She has been National Association
President and is currently Secretary to SI Republic of Ireland. She has rarely
missed a Federation Conference or International Convention. Retired from
Banking she is a sports fanatic – sailing, rugby and, of course, horse racing.
Recent mobility problems mean she is now just a keen supporter and is very
involved with the management of Sligo Yacht Club. Being an avid reader, keen
theatre goer and a bit of scribbling also keep her occupied!

Begging Letters

It seems like a dream. It was so long ago but a recent discussion on begging
letters dredged up the memory.

When I was seven I won £10 in a children's crossword in The Sunday Press. I
was contacted by the paper for a photograph and as I had just made my First
Communion, I duly sent off a picture of this angelic little lady. The following
Sunday there it was, my picture, full address and the fact that I had won the
princely sum of £10. £10 seemed a fortune to me then. Fame followed – every
relation and friend had read the good news and all were delighted.

However, there was a downside – I got dozens of begging letters – sad stories,
pleas to help our brethren in Africa and Asia. Who sent those letters? Was
there someone on 'winner watch' in all papers? Did they have a template of a
begging letter on file to dash off whenever they found a name and address? Did
they stop to think at all? Did they realise it was a seven year old that was the
recipient of this £10?

The letters kept coming. I cried about some of them – picked out two that I
was going to send £5 each. One was a mother who said her daughter was dying
and hoped to bring her to Lourdes and the other was for the starving children
in Biafra. I used to agonise about those letters that kept coming for about four
weeks. Then my parents took the matter in hand and explained to me that
many of the letters were bogus, but I was still upset.

They found a solution. I really lusted after a musical jewellery box that opened with a girl in a tutu dancing to music from 'Swan Lake'. This cost all of £8. The purchase was made and I was given £2 to light candles in the church and assuage my feelings of guilt.

My friend Claire and I had a field day as we lit up three rows of candles in front of the statue of Our Lady. We were not religious but really basked in the warm glow that pervaded the church as we listed out our intentions. I can't remember what they were – but I'm sure one or two were granted!

Monica Barry (SI Sligo, Republic of Ireland)

Lois A Herman *is Coordinator of the Women's UN Report Network (WUNRN),
which is considered one of the largest and most active global gender resource
programs. WUNRN addresses the human rights, oppression and empowerment
of women and girls all over the world and operates a daily information service
that goes throughout the UN system and enters over three quarters of UN
countries. Lois is a Gender Specialist. She founded the WUNRN European
office in Italy. She speaks regularly at the United Nations and Conferences and
has received several awards. Lois is a member of Soroptimist International of
Greater Minneapolis, USA. She has also visited Soroptimist clubs in at least nine
countries. Lois is a widow and has four children.*

Mama, I'm Hungry

Mama, I'm hungry
My tummy hurts, especially at night.
My hair and skin are now so dry.
I am only eight years old.

My baby brother cries.
He is hungry, too.
You say your milk has stopped.
You need food and safe water.

Daddy died some months ago.
Villagers say he killed himself.
There were so many debts.
He tried to buy food for us.

You say I can't go to school.
I want to be a teacher.
You send me work with bricks.
I am so tired, so very hungry.

The men look at me strangely.
They offer me food, candy.
They are rude. I am afraid.
But I am so hungry, Mama.

You married off my big sister.
Now one less mouth to feed here.
But I know she's not happy.
Her eyes are sad and full of fear.

Mama, I'm often cold at night.
I want food to keep me warm.
To cover me, you give me paper.
The hunger pangs won't let me sleep.

Will we lose our house as well?
Without home and land, can we survive?
I am so very hungry, Mama.
Can we really stay alive?

Will I grow up? I am not so sure.
I get very sick. I cannot play.
You talk about the big city.
But once there where would we stay?

I have hopes and I have dreams.
They seem so far away.
Like our food, dreams disappear.
I can only hope and pray.

Mama, I'm Hungry!

Lois Herman (SI Greater Minneapolis, Minnesota, USA)

Ann Truscott *has lived and worked in the Middle East and Africa. She is a former Probation Officer and Divorce Court Welfare Officer. She instigated the Mediation Project in Cornwall in 1998 (ACCORD MEDIATION) and worked on it until 2006. Ann became a Soroptimist in 1996 and was President of St Austell and District, Cornwall, England, in 1999. Ann is a mother, grandmother and step-grandmother. She is supposed to be retired now, with her farmer husband, but they are both busy and involved with charities, community work, the family and the family business.*

"The Youth of Today"

Remember when WE were young – and we youngsters respected our parents? *(except when we told lies about going to our girlfriend's house, when in fact we were going to meet our boyfriend!)*

Remember how WE revered our schoolteachers? *(except there was the incident of making the maths teacher cry with our deliberate unruliness!)*

Remember how WE were sent out to play for the whole day – trusted to "be good" and "behave ourselves" – which we did of course *(except when we stole apples from the farmer, bullied young siblings in our care and tied neighbours' door knockers together!)*

Remember when WE were scared of policemen? *(except when we 'aped' the local 'Bobby' behind him as he walked down the street, and let down his bike tyres!)*

Remember when WE kicked our ball against the door of the local 'grumpy old man' and taunted him when he came out to remonstrate with us?

No – WE weren't hooligans – WE were just having fun!

WE didn't get ASBOs; Supervision Orders; Specialist Social Workers; Educational Psychologists; ADHD or Autism Spectrum investigations…

How deprived were WE?!

Try to feel sorry for "The Youth of Today".

Ann Truscott (SI St Austell, England)

TALES OF TRAVEL

Jacque Emery *was born in Herne Bay, Kent, England. She trained as a professional singer at the Royal Academy of Music in London and also has Diplomas in Drama from LAMDA and a Masters Degree in Theology and Education from Liverpool University. Jacque has worked as a teacher in a variety of schools, finally becoming a Deputy Head teacher of a Comprehensive school in Hertfordshire. In 1988 she became an Education Adviser for Drama, Music and Religious Education in the Metropolitan Borough of Sefton. She has been an external examiner for LAMDA since 1978 and also became an Ofsted School Inspector. Jacque is currently Syllabus Manager and Chief Examiner for LAMDA Examinations. She has written two books of poetry for children, various educational articles, play scripts, songs and contributed to a book on the history of Musical Theatre. Attracted by the International dimension of Soroptimism, she joined SI Bootle and was President from 2003-04. She moved nearer to London and is now a member of SI Canterbury, serving as President from 2011-12. She is currently President Elect for her Region of South East England. Jacque loves travel, photography and reading – when she has time! She is single and lives with two pampered Persian cats.*

Postcards

I am postcards from a lifetime's journey.
I gather dust in cupboards crammed with slide boxes, CDs, albums and loose photographs.

I am the ancient abbey of Crowland in whose crumbling ruins young love briefly blossomed with a fumbled kiss and a dress grass-stained with dew.

I am the depths of the Grand Canyon sliced by the Colorado River, baked into every shade of red in the heat of summer; the sheer majesty of creation.

I am the stillness and silence of the Masai Mara, looking down from ballooning heights on to a ballet of migrating wildebeest.

I am the hot breath of a rum-filled, velvet night in a Caribbean Christmas, where steel pans syncopated rhythms of 'Silent Night' and 'Feliz Navidad'.

I am the tiger striding purposefully with strong, determined paws – beige-gold and black streaks through the long grass of Ranthambore. Inscrutable…and ageless.

I am the golden tints of sunrise warming the scrubland of the Gobi desert – spreading like ink over the vastness of the landscape as the train tumbles into day.

I am the torrential rain spilling over ankles, drenching every sodden article of clothing – splashing through the streets of Florence to the haven of an even wetter bus.

I am the mariachi band, the Mongolian throat singer, the Hawaiian ukulele, the harmonies of a Fijian highland church choir and the soaring Butterfly in Sydney Opera House. I am the grubby boy with a smile to split my face, singing my national anthem with my friends at Hermanus… my cap overflowing with appreciation from whale seeking tourists. 'Nkosi Sikilel' iAfrica'.

I am the excitement of an indrawn breath at the sheer beauty of the Taj Mahal. I am the shared exhilaration of fireworks whizzing, buzzing, flashing into starbursts lighting up the Madeiran sky and welcoming in another year.

I am the love that lasted little longer than the sunburn from an interminable cricket match. I am the snatched moment of intimacy on a wine-dark night in a Venetian gondola.

I am smiles…I am tears…I am exhaustion…I am laughter.

I am the luggage of half a century of travels.

I am memory.

Jacque Emery (SI Canterbury, England)

Heather Nestel *was born in East Sussex, England and in 1954 qualified as a veterinary surgeon from the Royal Veterinary College in London. After a period working on the college staff she went with her husband to Jamaica where they lived for nearly ten years and had three children. Heather built up a large mixed practice covering the northern half of the island. Her husband then joined the staff of the United Nations and during the next 12 years the family lived in Colombia (twice), Canada and Italy. During these years, as the opportunities arose, Heather gained a Masters degree in Pathology, practiced veterinary medicine and taught veterinary and medical students. In 1976 the family returned to the UK and Heather built up a large mixed practice in Redhill, Surrey from which she retired in 1990. The family then spent five years in Holland with Heather working as a consultant for IATA, playing a lead role in the development of international standards for the airline industry to follow for the safe and humane transport of all types of living animals. Throughout her career Heather has maintained an active and participatory interest in equine sports through playing polo in Jamaica, show jumping in the UK and Colombia, dressage in Holland and finally, in carriage driving in the UK. She is RDA Kent County Chairman and active as an instructor and assessor. Heather has been a Soroptimist since 1979 and a member of the clubs in Redhill, The Hague and Ashford. She has been President of both Redhill and Ashford – where she is now a member.*

Nothing Ventured, Nothing Gained!

An early memory from Jamaica, after arriving there in 1955, was that of carrying out my first major surgical operation under rustic conditions. My husband, Barry, was taking up a post of Veterinary Officer in the Ministry of Agriculture and I was going to work for the local equivalent of the RSPCA after we had spent a few weeks based in Kingston awaiting the birth of my first child and getting acclimatised. We were both 1954 veterinary graduates and I had spent the past year working as a house surgeon at the Royal Veterinary College.

On this particular morning Barry had gone to the foothills of the Blue Mountains to attend a cow that was having difficulty calving. I remained in the Veterinary Department being sociable and seeing how the Central Laboratory operated. While there I received a call from the office that Barry had requested

me to join him and to bring with me appropriate surgical equipment in case a
Caesarean section on the cow was required.

I do not remember taking any protective clothing such as rubber calving gowns
or gloves, not that the latter were usually worn at that time, but set off to meet
him with a set of hot sterilised instruments beside me in a car driven by one of
the veterinary support staff. We got to the foothills and came to a small crowd
by the roadside waving at us. Beside the road was a recumbent cow with a child
at its head and Barry looking very serious at its tail. He was obviously relieved
to see me and explained that there was a large calf inside a small cow and
sought my views as to what we should do as the roadside was not the optimal
location for abdominal surgery in the open air. I made a quick assessment of
the situation and decided that a Caesarean was the only feasible option. Fine,
I thought, until Barry asked me what type of anaesthetic I proposed to use?
Then the penny dropped, hard, that I had been invited to come to perform the
operation!

We had been taught at veterinary college 'nothing ventured nothing gained'
and as I had performed several bovine Caesareans during my time working in
the surgery department I could hardly say no. My bump was not the smallest
thing to work around but try I would. Water, soap and buckets were provided
from somewhere and I scrubbed up. By this time the road was obliterated by a
huge local audience who had arrived to see the action, and space was cleared
for the cow and me. One kind man went and cut two large banana leaves which
he held over me to give shade from the tropical sun. I can remember being so
grateful for this practical act of kindness and I used similar shade on a number
of occasions when working as a vet in the tropics.

The operation went smoothly, but it was not very comfortable for me nor, I
suspect, for the cow. Jamaicans enjoy betting and as it got closer to the time
of delivery the odds offered as to whether the cow or I would give birth first
became shorter and shorter. Fortunately for me the cow won and, somewhat to
my surprise, it had a live heifer calf and my reputation was made, both locally
and within the Ministry. The cow survived, and our daughter hung on for
another week, before becoming the first of my three Jamaican children.

Heather Nestel (SI Ashford, England)

One Good Turn Deserves Another

When I first went to Jamaica in 1955 there was an on-going major outbreak of poliomyelitis but limited resources available to deal with it. I was staying near to a large hospital awaiting the birth of my first child and met a number of the medical consultants socially. One of them, John, was an orthopaedic surgeon who had become very involved in establishing a Rehabilitation Centre for polio patients.

One evening he called the very pregnant me to ask for some help. A prominent local businessman had asked if John could do anything to help with his wife's dog which had broken its back leg. There were no small animal surgical facilities available in the island at that time and John was asked if he could set the dog's leg. He was accustomed to dealing with leg fractures, but not in animals, and had no experience of anaesthesia and post-operative care in dogs, nor any legal right to practice animal surgery. He asked me if I could be of help were he to make appropriate facilities available. He would not normally intervene in a veterinary matter but wanted to help if he could since the dog's owners had already provided substantial financial support for the Rehabilitation Centre and were discussing additional support as the Centre still lacked key facilities.

It was a delicate situation because apart from the animal welfare issue there was no question of the hospital authorities allowing an animal into an operating theatre, but the hospital desperately needed additional funding for the Rehabilitation Centre. We talked it over and decided that the only way to do the job was to return to the hospital after 10pm when the night staff would have taken over and got things settled for the night and the theatres would be cleaned, ready for the next day. We would then have to repeat the standard clean up after we had finished.

We made our plan for that night. The owner was to go to the staff car park just after 10pm. John would go earlier to the outpatient's surgical unit, where there was a small but adequate theatre, and collect the required sterile instruments, pins, wires and drapes etc. Being an outpatient area there were clippers available and of course all the cleaning fluids and disinfectants that we could possibly need. Luckily I had the correct anaesthetic for the procedure and so we were just hopeful that no one would see us and the dog!

John met up with me at the due time. Fortunately it was a very dark night with little moon. We found the owner and dog as planned and got into the hospital without being discovered. The dog was a standard poodle, a perfect patient who was very cooperative. Working together John and I pinned the fracture, aligning the bone perfectly, and returned a sleepy dog back to its owner in about an hour. We thought we had done a really good job covering our tracks and we all went our separate ways feeling very happy, including the dog and his owner.

A few days later John told me, the theatre sister had spotted the used vial of anaesthetic and the syringe in which it had been used. This was *not* hospital equipment and she was on the warpath. *Who* had been in her theatre? *What* had they been doing? *Where* were any patient records and *where* was the patient who had needed surgery with no record being made of follow up care? Apparently all staff were closely questioned but no one knew anything of this mysterious happening. John felt that he was under great suspicion as he was the bone surgeon and he finally confessed to his crime. He explained, without details, that he was the guilty party and had acted in the expectation of a generous donation towards the polio Centre. After he had been duly chastised peace prevailed.

Some weeks later there was a staff meeting to disclose a very large donation from the owner of the poodle towards setting up a dedicated polio Rehabilitation Centre within the hospital grounds.

There is a nice epilogue to this story in that several years later, when the work of the Rehabilitation Centre and its adjunct facilities had received international recognition, John received a knighthood from the Queen for his services to medicine in Jamaica.

Heather Nestel (SI Ashford, England)

Pat Fergusson *was brought up in Skipton, Yorkshire, England. She has always been fascinated by people, their words and language, word-play and the way in which humour changes according to place, culture and tradition. As an art teacher, Pat taught ceramics, changing direction to management training and latterly working as an English Language lecturer. Now living on the Lancashire coast, Pat's love of language continues when she is called upon as a proof-reader, an increasingly unpopular yet essential role as punctuation and grammar are neither sexy nor greatly used as electronic communication takes over. She also dabbles in poetry writing, recently being published and viewing verse as a subtle way of evening scores instead of getting annoyed! Pat joined SI Chorley in 1997 where she became President in 2005-06. The club closed and she transferred to SI The Fylde where she was President in 2009-10. She has recently completed three years as Membership Officer of the North West England and Isle of Man Region. Home life involves a motley group of adult children and grandchildren and care of her distant aunt in Manchester, who features in 'The Godmother'. Loving the outdoors and the tremendous variety in England's climate and countryside, Pat's leisure time is spent long-distance fell walking and gardening. She has just completed a half marathon to celebrate 25 years of pounding the streets, regarding running as her 'best friend', keeping her 'on the level in every sense of the word'.*

Professor Gao

Professor Gao was the personification of modest dignity and elegance. His position at a prominent Chinese University commanded respect from all who came within his elevated and academic orbit; students, parents, colleagues.

Touring in China and visiting the university, I met Professor Gao who was presiding over interviews. I wanted to shower and change my clothes after a day of travelling out of doors in the springtime heat and dust, but it was expected that I was briefly introduced to the Professor as I also worked in a similar field.

I considered my old leggings and faded green t-shirt less than suitable for this introduction. Professor Gao, tall and reed thin, watchful and serious, was beautifully attired in an impeccable suit and waistcoat, understated and refined down to the last detail, matched by his perfect manners and gracious welcome. I felt it was rather insulting to him that I looked as ragged as I felt but, unfortunately, there was no chance to slide away to spruce up.

After the introduction, I thought that I could reasonably excuse myself but was astonished to find that I was expected to sit through the interviews. Several hours later, the interviews over, Professor Gao took my hand, bowed and said, "I should be honoured if you would eat with me in my rooms here on the campus. You will be the guest of myself and my daughter, Kitty".

I hope my face was blank and polite to conceal the horror I felt at his kind invitation for which I was most inappropriately dressed, ill-prepared and slightly wary. "I must have a word with my colleagues. I believe we have plans", I replied.

"No matter, you must all be my guests", suggested Professor Gao.

And so it was, the traditional invitation to me from Professor Gao who regarded me as an equal in seniority to himself and therefore necessitating such hospitality. We repaired to his rooms, beautifully furnished in traditional Chinese style, calm and quiet with the Professor and his beautiful young daughter, Kitty, in attendance. She was dressed in a traditional cheongsam, perfectly groomed and acted as hostess. Their three guests looked a motley group, by comparison, casual and dusty and although perfectly respectable, this was one of those times where appropriate dress really did matter.

Two maids brought menus written in Mandarin for me, as the most senior of the guests of honour, to choose from. "It looks wonderful. Please, you choose", was the best I could manage.

Many plates of food, all beautifully decorated and presented were placed before us on the round table laid with shining glassware and plates. Tiny glasses of liquor were poured and toasts made, the conversation being quite stilted and without the familiarity of common ground. My dexterity with the chopsticks was not up to my usual standard, feeling at a disadvantage on every conceivable level. I was ill at ease, unprepared and wondered what would happen next, knowing that Professor Gao was doing all this through the professionalism of his position and good manners. We all gave our best performances but I believe that none of us wanted to be there.

The centrepiece of the banquet was a platter of marinated bananas, sliced longways, slippery and glossy, each set with a clam in the centre. With our chopsticks, the banana had to be picked up, dipped into a bowl of mayonnaise-like sauce, then brought to the mouth. The sequence struck fear into me, imagining the slimy texture of the banana shooting off in the direction of Professor Gao's perfectly hand-stitched lapels or Kitty's pristine dress. Astonishingly, the banana was duly eaten with greatest care and no disasters occurred, the banquet readily enjoyed and many movements made to my plate and napkin to cover the spillages in front of me. All in all, we had survived the rituals without embarrassing ourselves and finally said our goodbyes.

Chinese etiquette dictates a formal letter of thanks which I sent to Professor Gao and Kitty a few days later. His demeanour and hospitality were truly impressive and if he had been horrified about his guest's sartorial choices that day, he certainly did not show it. My thank you letter suggested that if ever Professor Gao and his family were in the UK, then I would be honoured to return the hospitality I had 'enjoyed'. To my relief, this has never presented me with the dilemma of how to host a comparable evening for such a charming man.

Pat Fergusson (SI The Fylde)

The Macau Guide Book

"We would like a twin room," we said, arriving in Macau at the traditional Chinese hotel described in the guide book.

"No room. Full," replied the receptionist and the manager agreed. This seemed unlikely on a cold and wet afternoon before Easter, so we persisted with our request. As I produced my credit card, the manager studied it hard and then said he had one room we could share, fifth floor at the back, no meals, no lounge or dining room. It was clean, quiet and good value.

Returning that evening from hours of exploration, the quiet hotel was transformed into a bright and busy bar and meeting place, music playing and the air of an old-fashioned dance hall pervaded. We took the lift to our room and shortly afterwards left the hotel by the same route for dinner in town.

As we left the hotel, my friend whispered, "It's a knocking shop. Look." "Never!" I exclaimed and then saw that the 'breakfast room' was a bar and waiting area and adjacent to the reception area we could peek into the handsome salon where a line of lovely and glamorous young girls stood in line. Yes, we were staying in a brothel!

It seemed that the staff initially thought we may be investigative journalists or police but realising that we were harmless enough, took our booking. Now we had the measure of our hotel, we found it fascinating: the clockwork comings and goings, the cool detachment of the young women and the shifty, cigarette smoking men who never looked anybody straight in the eye, it seemed.

We referred to the guide book again which promised a traditional hotel full of charm and interest. It wasn't until a couple of weeks later that we bought a new and updated copy of The Rough Guide to Macau and found a newer and more appropriate entry for our hotel: *"Formerly authentic and traditional lodging in the Chinese style of Old Macau, this once-charming hotel is now over-run by prostitutes. Avoid at all costs."*

Pat Fergusson (SI The Fylde, England)

Hilary Semple *became a Soroptimist in 1981 and has served on many Executive Committees. On the Management Board of Soroptimist International of South Africa, she has held a portfolio called National Editor (writing articles on major South African projects for The Soroptimist) and has also been Friendship Link Coordinator for South Africa. At the end of 1999 Hilary retired from the University of the Witwatersrand, Johannesburg, where she was a Senior Lecturer in English Literature. She is the ongoing editor of a Shakespeare Series and a founder member of the Shakespeare Society of Southern Africa. At the moment Hilary is involved with the University of the Third Age, where she has been giving a course on Shakespeare's plays. Hilary lives in a flat in a leafy suburb called Riviera – Johannesburg lies in the largest man-made forest in the world. She is single, goes to art classes, and enjoys being with her friends.*

The Delhi Diner, Johannesburg

Over coffee we observe
sober hijab heads go by,
and brilliant saris wrapped
round broad hips, burdened by
shopping bags, and near-noon
weariness;

behind a barrier of
plastic flowers and vines
laden with bunches of black
grapes (the Prohibition –
*no alcohol consumed
on these premises),*

the senses drink the heady
mix of movement and colour
and the ferment of sound,
until strangely light-headed,
we pay our bill, and leave

intoxicated.

Hilary Semple (SI Johannesburg, South Africa)

Patel's Shop: Indian Bazaar

Inside
the cool dimness
sequined scarves
hang like banners
their fringes moving
on currents of
air and incense;
pot-bellied cushions
like benign satin cats
with many mirror eyes
share shelves with
beaded silken slippers
from the Arabian Nights.

Did Sinbad sail this way?

Outside,
the car park,
tar acrid in the nostrils,
hot metal blinding
eyes narrowed in the sun:

there is only a short step
from one reality to another.

Hilary Semple (SI Johannesburg, South Africa)

The Traveller's Guide to Eyes
(For my brother, Roderick)

The impressions and memories of eyes are the most significant souvenirs gathered in one's travels. Collect what you will – key-rings or paperweights, scarves or hand-made scented candles, nothing beats a collection of eyes remembered with delight and astonishment.

I started my collection years ago in Madrid. Thick glossy eyebrows, which could have been hatched onto the forehead by the pen of an artist, set off dark eyes to dramatic advantage. The intensity of the *Madrileno* eye can be seen in paintings in the Prado. El Greco's noblemen dressed and ruffed sombrely, set in their gilt frames, catch the viewer's eye and hold it with a proud and solemn severity – not altogether unlike the bus driver who failed to understand the mispronounced Spanish in my request for directions that morning.

Specialist collectors of dark eyes can do no better than travel down to Andalucía, a southern kingdom whose name, I am told, means 'two steps from paradise'. Here eyes shine like divine black olives.

At the furthest northern extreme from Spain, in Norway, eyes capture the colours of fjord and sky and sea. These eyes reflect the long summer days of the far north and the blue-mauve hours of the day's long-drawn-out decline. They belong among waters and wild flowers, and the same hues were probably once seen in the enchanted eyes of the fairy creatures who lived in the mountains and birch forests a great while ago.

There are other eyes that belong to the world of waters – the sea. But another sea. The *Mare Nostra* of the ancient world, the sea we know as the Mediterranean. In it a special island. Sicily. The tides of history flowed onto its shores and sank into its soil. And its peoples carry in their bloodstreams the currents of Sicily's history – the ancient genes of the Mediterranean world. One current brought with it turquoise green eyes the colour of the sea close to shore. These eyes are as clear as the pooling water, revealing the refraction of blue-green light. They are sometimes cool or unfathomable, and always beautiful. The Sirens must have had such beguiling eyes when they sang to sailors long ago.

If you stand in the ancient Greek Theatre at Taormina and look through the vault of sky and sea to Naxos, it is not difficult to imagine the storm-tossed wanderer, Prince Odysseus, sailing in those waters with his sea-filled eyes. Many years, many landfalls, so many crashing waves. So much blue-green to leave behind him in his wake.

Travelling on to Turkey. Few places can offer such riches to the connoisseur of eyes. These eyes descend from the nomadic warrior tribes that made their homes in the green stillness of the mountains and in the valleys leading down to the plains.

I have collected two famous specimens here. The celebrated hazel eye and the black eye, both praised in epic poetry from past centuries, and encountered on the banks of the Bosphorus, the bazaar at Izmir, or in small villages in the Anatolian mountains. The hazel eye is a collector's item, having a cinnamon-brown and copper base and flecks of olive green like the wheel formation in a kaleidoscope radiating out from the pupil. In sunlight these eyes have a green-amber glint; at night the glow of polished bronze.

The dark eye has a lovely almond shape, a unique contour. In the *Book of Dede Korkut,* when two great Khans lamented, they cried tears of blood from their black almond eyes! Apparently it was customary to scratch the face to convey great sorrow, and blood mingled with tears. But I prefer to believe that the great Khans wept tears that came from their hearts' blood, and that these tears of blood welled up richly red in their black almond eyes to roll heavily down their cheeks. What a dramatic spectacle!

In Greece I looked for an eye I have never seen – other than in my imagination. One hot afternoon in Delphi, I scrambled through undergrowth and olive trees looking for the god Pan. He lives in woody places. Had I found him, he would have stared at me like a leopard, with flaring yellow eyes, two spirals into which one could fall in a sudden attack of vertigo and panic before running away. Or not. Perhaps stay and listen to him play his pan pipes.

Collecting much further east, the Thais have eyes that are elongated, shaped gracefully like willow leaves, and filled with shining living jet. They shine from bicycles and scooters, and along the crowded pavements of Bangkok, from tuk-tuks and sampans. Friendliness and curiosity give them a twinkle, which is the optical equivalent of the clear tinkle of temple bells.

For eyes that specialise in charm, it would be hard to outdo the claim of Italian or Irish eyes. Italian eyes are legendary for their amorous, seductive powers, and Irish eyes can smile and steal your heart away, as the song says. This congenial theft is as natural to the Irish as green is to grass, and the Cliffs of Moher to the Atlantic.

When it comes to collecting French eyes circumspection is necessary as it is in all things Gallic. Especially in Paris where one's interested stare might be greeted with *hauteur*. So my favourite pair of French eyes belongs to a fictional character, Madame Bovary. We read that in shadows her eyes are black, and in bright light they are dark blue and that beneath a shining surface there are layers of colour, which graduate to surface transparency. They are opaque and translucent: lustrous paradoxes! Very French.

A good spot for the amateur collector of eyes is Piccadilly Circus. A multitude of eyes of all shapes and sizes throng round Eros, who, precariously balanced on his column, is now the presiding deity of diversity. You may take your pick and lay the foundation of your collection. But among the crowds where is the quintessential English eye, or more correctly perhaps, the British eye? At a hazard I would say in the National Gallery, where ironically a Spaniard, Francisco Goya, painted a slightly protuberant blue eye on the face of the Duke of Wellington, who was of Anglo-Irish descent, and who defeated Napoleon (not a Frenchman but a Corsican) at Waterloo, which is in Belgium not France. Peoples and places and victories are contained in his gaze! Wellington's eye is self-assured as befits a military chest covered with medals!

The Americas, like parts of Africa, replicate the eyes of east and west. But the southern part of Africa is unique. Highveld eyes are either very ancient or modern – ancient because the Cradle of Mankind, Maropeng, is situated here. These eyes contain the dark midnight shadows of humanity's long history, descending from those first humans, who wandered upright over the veld. Different eyes survived the storms where the Atlantic meets the Indian Ocean, and arrived at Cape Town, the Tavern of the Seas. They came marauding inland aglitter for yellow gold and the sparkle of diamonds. So a very ancient past and a recollected present meet and mingle.

But enough of my collection! The world is wide, and there are many more eyes waiting to be caught in a glance and a gaze, to become a memory for delight and reflection.

Hilary Semple (SI Johannesburg, South Africa)

Hannah Lurie *studied part-time at Natal Technical College from 1956-61 under the tutelage of the sculptress, Mary Stainbank. She is a resident of Durban, South Africa and is a poet and a well-known sculptor. She has held numerous solo exhibitions in Durban, Cape Town, Johannesburg and Pretoria, and her work can be seen in many corporate and public galleries throughout South Africa. Her last piece was of two 9ft. tall bronze figures. Hannah is also a cancer survivor and she has written a book entitled 'I'm too sexy for my hair' of which 26,000 copies have been circulated free of charge. She received the Mariette Loots Award for this publication. Hannah also won two national poetry competitions, Waterman Pen and Adams Books. Inducted as a Soroptimist in 1972, she is a Past President of the Durban Club as well as Past President of Soroptimist International of South Africa. Hannah has three sons, one in Johannesburg, one in London and one in Ghana.*

Sleeping Paris
(Paris, September 2006)

I wake up,
my bedside clock says 4am.
It's not the kind of waking
when a trip to the bathroom
means back to slumber time,
nor have I woken from a bad dream –
It's wide awake wake up.
I throw off the blanket
open my curtains
and look at sleeping Paris.
Full moon –
The moon glints mirrors
onto the Seine through the poplars
I look down to the pavement.
On a bench, a homeless man, a clochard –
smokes a cigarette and drinks from a bottle.
Now he draws an enormous length
of tin foil over himself.
Somehow he manages to tuck himself in –

Bizarre
He looks like a wrapped whale
waiting for the freezer
or perhaps with tomatoes and onions
and a soupcon of garlic
waiting for the oven.
In the background, I see the
shadow of the Pantheon
and the Notre Dame to the right.
I draw the curtains
pull up the sheet
and wait for sleep

Hannah Lurie (SI Durban, South Africa)

Barbara Milburn *was born in Lower Hutt, New Zealand. After graduating from Victoria University College she had a career in education as a teacher, School Principal and Lecturer in English at the Wellington College of Education. Along the way, she and her husband Jim, with two teaching friends, formed Price Milburn and Co, a successful Educational Publishing Company which won a New Zealand Export Pennant in 1974 and for which she edited a series of Cookbooks and Studies in New Zealand Literature. After leaving teaching she travelled the World as Sales Manager for the company. Barbara has been a Soroptimist for 27 years and is at present Publicity Officer for SI Upper Hutt. She is a regular contributor to the Soroptimist Chatline. Presently retired she is patron of the Upper Hutt Animal Rescue Society and very much enjoys the company of her cat Ginger. Barbara and Jim are regulars at Soroptimist Events within New Zealand and Barbara was at the recent South West Pacific Federation Conference held at Greymouth.*

Blackout

Headlines from the New York Times, Friday 15 July 1977

NEW YORK'S POWER RESTORED SLOWLY. LOOTING WIDESPREAD. 2,700 ARRESTED. BLACKOUT RESULTS IN HEAVY LOSSES.

My husband and I were staying in Yonkers, New York with New Zealand friends. They had left for a week for their beach house on Long Island and we were alone in New York.

The weather was extremely hot and sultry. We came into the city by train that Thursday and spent the day on business, had dinner and went on to the Broadway production of *A Chorus Line*. In the middle of the performance, around 9.45pm, the theatre lights went out. The audience sat still, waiting. Eventually, the manager came on stage and announced that there was a complete power failure in New York; he was closing the theatre and everyone would have to leave.

We were concerned – how would we get back to Yonkers? Where would we stay the night? We were discussing whether we should seek out a church for sanctuary when an elderly gentleman who had overheard our conversation grabbed our arms and said he would take us across the city to the Robert Taft Hotel where he was staying. He had come down from Washington for the show.

What a kindly gentleman he was. Firmly holding our hands he guided us through the crowded streets of Broadway's red light district to the hotel on Seventh Avenue. The darkness was pierced intermittently by torchlight from the teenagers who had taken over the intersections and were guiding the snail like traffic flow.

At the hotel scores of people were already jammed into the foyer. Some were hotel guests unable to get to their rooms because the elevators had stopped, others like us, were refugees from the street and a number were airline crews unable to reach the airport. There were no lights of course, but by this time enterprising hawkers had appeared selling light sticks. I settled on the floor for the longest night of my life. It was swelteringly hot. From time to time burly guards escorted ladies in convoy to the toilets on the first floor where there was a dreadful stench as the toilets could not be flushed. My husband went with the males which was even scarier as he was apprehensive that he might be attacked at any time. We could hear transistor radios reporting severe rioting in the streets and outlying areas and every now and again gun toting policemen came into the hotel to check that we were all right.

Gradually, we became aware of the terrifying situation outside. In many buildings people were being cut from lifts which had stopped between floors, petrol pumps were having to be worked by hand, trains were stopped because the tunnel under the Hudson river had flooded when the pumps stopped, subway passengers had to evacuate trains and walk the tracks in the darkness, rioting and looting was rife, millions of dollars of frozen food rotted in the freezers, emergency hospital generators failed. The Mayor went on air to declare the city a disaster area and tell everybody they were not to attempt to come into the city to work the next day.

The night dragged on forever. All I wanted was to get on the next flight back to New Zealand. When daylight came we exited the hotel onto the streets of a completely deserted city. We were lucky to find a cab back to Yonkers where we found to our relief that our friend had come back from Long Island when he heard of the blackout. He restored our sanity and we waited out the restoration of power over the next 24 hours or so with him, making meals on the garden barbeque.

Even now when I look back on the experience I have a scary feeling. Not panic perhaps but just bewilderment. What do you do in the centre of a city like New York at night when the lights go out and everything stops? Knowing no one, unaware of the escape routes, physically tired, hot and sticky in the humid atmosphere, surrounded by looters, rioters and tetchy armed policemen. Without the intervention of the kindly stranger from Washington, who knows?

Barbara Milburn (SI Upper Hutt, New Zealand)

Mary McCormick *was born in Cricklade, Wiltshire, England. She left home at the age of 15 to train as a Nursery Nurse with the Church of England Children's Society, now The Children's Society. This was the first step in a life of working in the NHS as a nurse, eventually becoming a Health Educator and Project Manager. Mary worked in The Gambia, Romania, Bosnia and Cameroon, West Africa – the latter from 2000-11. Some of this work was as a volunteer with Voluntary Service Overseas (VSO). Mary spent the last 10 years running a charity in Cameroon. She has two children and six grandchildren. She joined the Soroptimist club in Lancaster four years ago and was Joint President with another member. It was a move that worked well. Mary loved travel, fell walking, music, opera, gardening and reading. Mary passed away on 10 July 2013.*

To Be a Pilgrim

The train was moving fast, taking me from the South of England to the North. I was enjoying watching the countryside flash by. England looked beautiful; fields, trees, hedges – all a wonderful green. Cows, sheep and horses were dotted around in the fields. The sky was blue, the sun was shining, my head was in the clouds and all was peaceful in my world.

A few words from the passenger sitting next to me broke through my mood and listening to her story changed my life. For the next three years I thought about the tale she told me until I felt I had to stop thinking and start 'doing'.

In my mind I called the talkative passenger 'Sparrow' because she reminded me of that chirpy bright little bird. An elderly lady, 75 she told me later, no more than four feet ten inches tall, very thin with an almost fully shaved head that just sported enough hair to look as if she had a silver sheen all over her scalp; her large dark brown eyes sparkled with fun. Her opening remark was "Can you open these damned sandwiches for me my dear, arthritic fingers make it impossible for a person to open the wretched thing". The sandwiches in question were the type found in many shops – the ones packed tight in a triangle shape fastened down with plastic covers hard even for normal fingers to open. "I really must write to someone about it" she continued and with that she passed the offending packet to me which I dutifully opened and handed back.

After munching away on one half of the sandwiches Sparrow pushed them away from her, leant back on the seat and cheerfully announced she was bored with just sitting all the time so would I tell her something about myself. Somewhat taken aback at this approach I mumbled some mundane activities I was involved in not really wanting to get drawn into an inconsequential conversation with a stranger. Sparrow interrupted me by saying, "Oh come on my dear, just do something interesting whilst you are young enough." I was coming up to 70 at the time. She continued, "For instance get on a bike and just go somewhere. I did that very thing a few years ago and have never regretted the adventure".

Intrigued by now I asked her to tell me about her, quote "bike ride going somewhere".

"To Santiago de Compostela" she said casually. Now I was really hooked as it was one of the places to visit on my bucket list. "Go on", I said. "Why, when, how?" Her eyes twinkled and leaning her tiny head back on the seat she began to tell her tale.

"My husband was a diplomat" she began, "which meant we travelled a lot – something I really enjoyed. Sadly he died ten years ago and since that time I have been going to Lourdes every year as a volunteer helping with disabled people who wished to make the Pilgrimage to the healing waters of Bernadette's grotto next to the Gave de Pau River. The last time I went" she continued, "I thought to myself, here I am footloose and fancy free. Why don't I do something else while I am here? Thinking of the Lourdes pilgrims brought to mind the fact I was staying near the beginning of one of the routes originally walked by the disciples of the Apostle James. They wanted to make a pilgrimage to visit the tomb of their leader who had been buried in the Cathedral in Santiago after being executed under the reign of King Agrippa I. So my dear with no more ado I made up my mind to do a pilgrimage of my own from Lourdes, France to Santiago Cathedral, Spain." Sparrow went very quiet for a few moments. I interpreted her slight smile as a smile of remembrance so I said nothing until she was ready to continue.

With a little shake of her head she began to talk again as if she had not paused at all. "Of course I had no idea of how to get from Lourdes to Santiago so I found a shop that sold me a map of the area which I studied by tracing my finger along the route I needed to take. Oh my, I thought that's a long way to walk. It will take six weeks or more. I will go and buy a bicycle which will take half the time." I laughed.

"And did you?" I asked.

"Of course I did" she replied, "and I also bought a couple of panniers, put in four t-shirts, one for each of the three weeks, the time I thought it would take me to complete the pilgrimage, and one clean one for when I got there. Two pairs of shorts, six pairs of knickers, three pairs of socks and a bar of soap was all I would need. Water and food I would buy on the way. Oh yes, I put in a couple of books of the areas I would be going through to read when I would be lying on a bunk in an auberge unable to sleep as I was sure there would be a lot of snorers in the same room."

"What about washing your clothes?" I queried.

Sparrow chortled. "Ha, I just threw them away when they became too dirty to wear, a good way to lighten the load."

I was totally engrossed by this time, as I really could not imagine such a tiny elderly little lady going off on a whim, undertaking a journey most people would plan for weeks ahead. The idea of sharing bunk beds in a basic room with other pilgrims just did not seem to go with someone who was used to the life of a diplomat's wife. Sparrow was chuckling to herself at my obvious surprise. "Go on", I said. "What happened next?"

"Well my dear what I had not fully taken into account was the fact that my journey took a route over the Pyrenees mountains and as I had not ridden a bike for ten years this fact did become a bit of a worry to me."

"So what did you do about it?" I asked.

"What do you think I did?" she replied. "I pushed the bike over the hills and mountains. In fact I pushed it most of the way – which was rather a waste of money come to think of it. However" she continued, "I was determined I would arrive pedalling the bike and ride it into the Cathedral square and that is exactly what I did." Another pause as she gave rein to the memory of her entrance as a pilgrim into the magnificent square of the Cathedral. She continued, "I rode through head held high as I looked at the awe inspiring front of the Cathedral only stopping to ask one of the policemen walking around the square to direct me to the best hotel in town. He looked at me oddly and pointed to a very grand building in a leafy area to the side of the square. "For you?" he said raising his eyebrows. I know I looked a sight, dirty, dishevelled and very tired but after all I was a pilgrim." She grinned impishly and went on, "I ignored the policeman's implied criticism and rode off up the drive to the beautiful wooden doors of the hotel frontage. I learned later it had once been a monastery. A doorman stood watching me with his mouth open and a look of disdain on his face. Disregarding his obvious misgivings of having to talk to me I rode as near to him as I dared, jumped off the bike, thrust the handlebars into the front of his tunic saying, "Get rid of this for me young man, I never want to see it again". He just stood there staring at the bike, then at me before he closed his open mouth, righted the bicycle and wandered off. I then stepped into the foyer of a beautiful but simple building and creaked my way up to the reception feeling a little stiff after walking and riding a long way during the past three weeks. Again I was looked at as if I was in the wrong place until I said in my best 'diplomat wife voice', "Give me the best room in the hotel, the best bath oils and fragrances you have and, in one hour's time send up a bottle of the very best wine – only one glass with it if you don't mind." Sparrow laughed at the memory. "Of course, flashing an American Platinum Gold card helped" she chuckled.

"You amaze me" I said, "Just doing all that on your own. Did the hotel give you everything you asked for?"

"Indeed yes", Sparrow replied. "I needed to change the bath water twice to wash away three weeks dirt and grime. After soaking up the oil and bubbles, I lay on the sumptuous bed and drank the whole bottle of extremely good wine they had brought up, leaving me feeling that all was well with the world. I then donned my last clean t-shirt, shorts had to stay dirty, then went off to pay my respects and give thanks to St. James at his tomb inside the Cathedral. This is a tradition a pilgrim is expected to do on completion of a safe journey. This act completed, I went to find the shopping area to buy some decent clothes. The next day I went to the Cathedral for the Pilgrim's service that was held three times a day for incoming pilgrims. Believe me when I tell you it was an amazing experience. In fact" she said looking me straight in the eye, "I am not going to tell you anymore about Santiago de Compostela. Go and experience it for yourself." And with that she went back to her sandwiches.

Four years later I did walk to Santiago de Compostela, not the route Sparrow took but the 160 mile route from Porto, Portugal through to Spain and eventually to Santiago.

A truly remarkable experience. But that is another story.

Mary McCormick (SI Lancaster, England)

The following two poems tell the stories of the clearances in Scotland and the subsequent travels of the people.

Diaspora

An ovine hourglass
poured
through the breached wall;

a hundred distinctive bleats
triangulating a new geography –
heafed on the hill
before the blackened hearths grew cold,
chevron molars grinding
the heart of the land against
bony palate.
Neat cloven hooves trampling
dandelion clocks
which once a child's fist
would pluck,
enquiring breath disperse:
yan tan tethera
for
aon dha tri.

Dispossessed, shepherdless
bone backed against bearded stone
skinned with thin machair,
bitter wind wrings brine from the stare
faced by the green sea –
wall or way
settle or sail?

Clare Harding (SI Blackburn, England)

Abandoned Croft-House

Weather has fretted
the ochred iron into lace,
which frays rain into beaded tassels.
Square-heads nail
air to the rafters,
the roof-tree a rowan
in full bloom.
Windows gape
at swallow-plastered cornices,
homespun blankets of
woolly hair-moss
drape the walls,
and fern flickers in the fireplace.

A rufous wing-blur of wren
announces visitors.

Clare Harding (SI Blackburn, England)

Meeting in Hiroshima, Easter 2002

Mary and I planned to meet by the Tourist Information Centre at Hiroshima Railway Station at 17:00 hours. I had travelled from Manchester UK to Tokyo earlier that day and was on time.

No Mary.

An hour later, enquiries revealed that there are two Tourist Information Centres at the station with an adjoining subway, a circuit of about 20 minutes between the two and which I plodded around repeatedly with no rendezvous.

Towards dusk and not knowing the city, I went to the Railway Police Kiosk. The Japanese policemen peered up from their break-time plates of noodles. You could see the exchanged look of horror – "European – lost – she's yours" – as they glanced sideways at each other.

Led by the tiny policeman, I was still dragging my luggage. He ushered me to a nearby large hotel where I booked in, rang home and left sensible messages in case Mary rang there – no mobiles at this time. Then I returned to the station and covered another few circuits between the Tourist Information Centres and, realising I was exhausted after an endless day, returned to the hotel to sleep, unsure what to do next.

The phone in the hotel bedroom rang. Mary.

"You're there, aren't you?"

We met, so relieved, in the hotel lobby. It seemed we had followed each other round the circuit all evening, presumably missing each other by moments. Then, at a loss, she resorted to the nearest international hotel to ring my UK home. In the reception area, she had seen the curious look of the receptionist who had been bemused to encounter two lone British women in as many hours, late on a damp and quiet Monday evening. Mary saw his expression. "She's here, isn't she?" Mary asked him. He nodded. "Room 1234. Ring her."

I have often wondered what would have happened if these massive coincidences had not rushed to our aid: both of us going to the same hotel, the quiet evening and the astute receptionist and the way we repeatedly missed each other at the station.

"Would you have stayed in Hiroshima or carried on with our plans?" I asked Mary.
"Carried on. What about you?"
"Stayed put", I replied.

So far from home and so many chances never to find each other. Fate smiled strongly on us that evening.

Pat Fergusson (SI The Fylde, England)

Ann Greenfield *was born in Barnet and spent her childhood in Hertford, England. On leaving school she trained as a teacher and taught in primary schools for most of her career. She obtained a degree through the Open University and a Diploma in Education at the University of Canterbury. She became a Soroptimist in 1992, joining SI Sevenoaks and later transferring to SI Tunbridge Wells and District where she now lives. Ann was Regional President of South East England in 2000-01, Regional Programme Action officer in 2004-08 and Region Ambassador for Project Sierra. She has been married to David for 46 years and they have two children and five grandchildren. Ann loves to travel and was lucky enough to visit Sierra Leone on one of the Project Sierra Study Tours in 2010. She is currently churchwarden at All Saints' Parish Church in Langton Green and sings with the Royal Tunbridge Wells Choral Society. Her hobbies include gardening, theatre, family history and reading.*

A Story for Peace

1945 – 1995. United Kingdom. Japan. Hiroshima and simple origami cranes.

August 1945: a little girl two years old was at home with her mother somewhere in Hertfordshire. Hostilities in Europe had ended bringing hope for a bright future. Her name was Ann.

August 1945: a little girl two years old was at home with her mother in Hiroshima. Her name was Sadako. Something indescribably terrible was about to happen.

November 1954: the young girl in the UK was now 11 years old and enjoying her first term at secondary school.

November 1954: in Hiroshima, the young 11 year old Japanese girl fell ill and was diagnosed with Leukemia. She was given just one year to live.

Sadako heard the traditional Japanese story that anyone who folds a thousand origami cranes will be granted a wish by the Gods. Her wish was that she would live. She began folding the origami cranes and continued until her death. Her wish was not granted – she died on 25 October. Her friends continued to fold the paper cranes, which have become a symbol of peace.

Her school friends raised funds for a memorial to Sadako and all the children who had died as a result of the atom bomb. This now stands in the Hiroshima Memorial Peace Park. The inscription reads:

This is our cry. This is our prayer. Peace in the world.

1995: this year was the 50th anniversary of the dropping of the A Bomb. A British woman aged 52 was enjoying a successful career, was married with a family. She travelled to Japan and was exploring the cities and visiting the sights. It was a mild sunny spring day as she walked through the Peace Park on her way to the Peace Memorial Museum. It was hard to imagine that almost 50 years before it had been the scene of such devastation.

The Sadako memorial was covered in what seemed to be a mass of coloured paper – thousands of origami cranes folded by the young people of Japan. Many were waiting their turn to have their photo taken by the statue. Groups of Japanese school children walking through the park were keen to engage with visitors, stopping to greet them and to ask questions. They thrust peace messages into the hands of passers-by. I still have mine.

Yes, I am Ann, that British girl born the same year as Sadako. I am the woman who went to Japan in 1995. My son was there on his gap year.

As I flew home a few days later I wiled away the hours reflecting on the experiences and sights I had enjoyed. I couldn't help wondering whether Sadako, as a 52 year old mother, might have been flying in the opposite direction having visited her son enjoying a gap year in England, had her life not been cut short – had she not been an innocent victim of war.

Ann Greenfield (SI Tunbridge Wells, England)

Mother of the Bride

When I received the wedding invitation I was reminded of an incident many moons ago. Auntie Pat, a teacher, was a great friend who lived beside us in Dun Laoghaire. She was a native of Belfast but had married a Dubliner. Her daughter Sinead was getting married and Auntie Pat decided to go to Belfast to get the 'Rig-Out' for the wedding. She had a day off school and decided to travel north on the train. At that time customs restrictions were very stringent and one wasn't allowed to bring anything back to the 'Free State'.

Auntie Pat was well aware of this and made her plans. All the clothes she would wear to Belfast could be discarded and she would don the new outfit and wear it back on the train. She dressed in a tweed skirt that had seen better days with the 'S' bend at the back. This was topped by a washed out pink twin set that she had been meaning to throw out. Over this fetching ensemble she wore one of those ghastly plastic raincoats with a hood. She was also wearing her scuffed driving shoes.

She set off and had a lovely peaceful trip to Belfast. Just as she emerged from Central Station and was about to make an onslaught on the shops, she bumped into a college friend from Queens. They chatted for a few minutes and he suggested they repair to a nearby hostelry for a drink. She was delighted. He and his wife had been very good friends of hers during their student days but had lost touch.

While in the pub, she caught sight of him eyeing her rather oddly in the mirror and decided to tell him her story – she was up to get an outfit for her daughter's wedding. Relief spread all over his face. He confessed that he thought she had fallen on hard times and was even going to offer her some money. He contacted his wife who joined them for lunch. They had such a good time reminiscing that she abandoned the whole idea of shopping. The booze would have clouded her decision making anyway!

She just made the last train back to Dublin. Sinead and her fiancé were somewhat taken aback at the dishevelled creature that embarked from the train at Amiens Street. She had enjoyed a fantastic day but there was nothing to show for it except memories.

The wedding outfit was eventually bought in a local store!

Monica Barry (SI Sligo, Republic of Ireland)

Mary Clarke *was born in Ashford, Kent, England. She qualified in medicine from the Royal Free Hospital, London in 1966 and after some years in Occupational Health for British Rail, went into General Practice for 30 years in a fairly deprived and multicultural practice in Croydon. In 1998 Mary re-qualified in Child Psychiatry at the Institute of Psychiatry. She retired from General Practice in 2002 and since then, has been thoroughly enjoying her work with children with behavioural problems in Croydon. Mary's husband was a graphic designer working for the Central Office of Information until 1993. They have two children – a daughter living in France with one daughter of her own, and a son in Oxford. Mary has been a member of SI Beckenham and District for over 20 years and has spent much of that time as recurrent Treasurer! She was President in 1994 and joint President again in 2010! In between work and Soroptimism, she enjoys gardening and renovating her small stone cottage in Normandy.*

Leaving

The call came as her husband was having breakfast. It was not unexpected but a cloud descended over daybreak and was reflected in the grey rain falling, as he looked out over the lawn towards the bare trees beyond.

The day before, he had taken a walk by the lake. It had been cold and frosty and the silver birches had shimmered in the early spring sun. The ground was hard and there was a slight crackle under foot as he stepped in old footprints of other walkers seeking solitude. It was his time to reflect and remember.

Looking through the undergrowth he could see sheets of ice still glistening in the shady areas of the water that the sun had yet to reach and in the distance a flock of geese growing restive as they prepared to move on. Suddenly the leader flapped its wings and, calling to its companions, rose into the air followed by others soon forming an orderly 'V' as they left the lake to find remembered feeding grounds on their journey north.

He would also have to travel north and his journey would also take him back to the familiar territory of his childhood. He would fly but it would be by budget airline after a hurried search for a suitably sombre tie, his identity papers and the interminable queues familiar to air travellers.

Usually on crossing the Irish Sea he could look down on the Isle of Man with the verdant hills of Antrim and the dark mass of Lough Neagh in the distance and feel a warm sense of homecoming, but not today. Cloud enveloped the plane and the land below.

Familiar landmarks flashed by as the coach entered the city bringing back memories of college days that had preceded his first departure for new horizons. Leaving the city that would go through destruction and conflict before its rebirth as a rejuvenated but wiser place, he would be the last of the siblings to leave to make a different life across the Irish Sea.

Now he was the last one able to return to mark the passing of the sister he had left behind so many years before. She had been the slender link with his home city so often shrouded in mist but surrounded by the hills and rivers enjoyed in their youth. She had been the connection with those early memories of soda bread, dulse and yellow man. She was the one to have revived and reconstructed the family myths and beliefs of childhood.

The sun made a hesitant appearance as though to lift the gloom and revive his affection for his homeland. It was time to say his farewell as the rituals of death and burial were performed but no-one present remembered those early days when they were close.

This time, after pausing for thought and rediscovery, he would be leaving, perhaps forever; flying south to 'move on' with life now more familiar.

Mary Clarke (SI Beckenham, England)

The following poem is a reflection on present and past train travel, an integral part of the stories of our lives.

Senior Railcard

like starlings
the unmated young
flutter
as they voice their wares,
broadcast love
on mobiles
in public glare.

long gone
the night-nestle
of compartments
whose wooden doors
guillotined the everyday;
a single
coat cloaked
nascent nakedness,
and travelling
was better
than to arrive.

Clare Harding (SI Blackburn, England)

TALES OF LIFE

Val Christoffersen *was born in London, England. At the age of ten her family moved to Cape Town, South Africa, where she now lives. During WWII she served in the South African Women's Auxiliary Naval Service (SWANS). Val sang professionally for 27 years in the Chorus of Cape Town's Opera Company CAPAB (Cape Performing Arts Board). She is a member of U3A 'Pleasure and Education' and has recently presented operas on DVD to interested members. Val has also specialised in Financial Planning, Estate Planning, Wills and Tax Planning and has spoken widely to groups of women on 'Women and Finance'. She was Manager of a branch of 'Syfrets' in Cape Town, a long-established historical Trust Company. She is a Founder of the Belmont Care Centre for Mentally Challenged young people and has run a Recreation Club for teenagers in this category. She has raised funds to buy a Residential Care Centre which now houses seven adults. Val married a Dane and lived in Denmark for a while, forming a special affinity for the country and its people. She reads, writes and speaks Danish. She is now a widow with two children and three grandchildren who live in Australia. Val has been a Member of SI Cape of Good Hope for many years and she has been Club President, Treasurer and Secretary. She has also been the Friendship Link Coordinator and has served on a sub-committee for the anti-trafficking of women and children. Val served for two years as National Secretary for Soroptimist International of South Africa (SISA). She received a 'Soroptimist of the Year' Award in 2006. Her hobbies include playing indifferent Bridge and Mahjong!*

Constance

People come in and out of our lives leaving varying impressions – some lasting and some difficult to recall. Because of the long life I have lived, the list of such impressions is equally long and varied, but one who comes to mind is Constance.

Constance arrived on my doorstep and I cannot remember who recommended her to be my weekly domestic help. It was always with some trepidation that one invited a new 'char' into one's home. Would she be honest? Would she be punctual? Would she break my possessions? South African women were very good at thinking negatively about the valued help that they could not do without. Attend any house party and there they would be in the corner decrying the latest misfortunes they had experienced at the hands of their 'servants'. The men, of course, would be in another corner discussing sport, clutching beers or brandies. Such was the social interaction of days gone by.

So here was Constance, short, solid and round, with a happy smile on her face showing brilliantly white teeth. She wasted no time and got on with her work with great energy. As time went by we began to open up to conversation, although such time together was limited initially as I had a job to go to and was grateful for the heavy domestic chores being taken off my hands. Constance told me of her husband who drank so much that he became violent and had seizures – a warning sufficient to make him give up the bad habit as he had a job which paid well and promised a payout when retirement came. I discovered that she lived in the male or bachelor quarters in Langa where married couples were not allowed. "But I dress behind a blanket, Medem, which I hang up and that is how we manage."

She had children in the Transkei who were being harried out of their schools by malcontents of that time. It was a restless time during the early 1980s. Every annual trip home in the December holidays was to see to new school uniforms, till her land and take advantage of the rains and build another room onto her home which she was preparing for the days of retirement. Ever resourceful, Constance would take back a large bag of dried beans with her which she sold to neighbours for one Rand per cup. The milk from her cow was given – "No, Medem, we don't sell our milk, we give it."

One day she shyly told me that her 17 year old school-going daughter had a baby – a little girl called Portia. "But the boy's parents must pay us". And so a happy negotiation of 1000 Rand was concluded. Nature being what it is, a year or two later her son performed the same miracle of creating life and so, she and her husband, in turn, had to pay the agreed amount to the girl's family.

Portia grew old enough to be handed over to her grandmother for rearing. I have no idea how she and her husband accommodated this child. Only that I suggested we get her to a nursery school in Observatory and that we share the cost of the fees. This worked very well even though Portia's cognitive skills were way behind those of other children of her age, simply because there had never been the stimulus that town children receive. My day for Constance was a Friday and it fell to me to fetch Portia from her school whilst Constance was working and when we passed the fish and chip shop on the main road in Mowbray, this little face would look up at me and say expectantly "Tjips?" Of course, we stopped for chips – how could one not. On arriving home her lunch would be ready and I had a thin foam rubber mattress which I had placed on the floor for her. "Now, Portia, you must 'lala' " I said, and whilst Constance finished her work, the little girl slept.

I had a call one day from the Minister of the church which ran the nursery school. He had taken to visiting the families of the children attending the school. "Have you seen where that child lives?" he asked of me indignantly. "No," I said. "I have not but that is why this child is attending your nursery school."

Anecdotes and stories of Constance are too many to be told but the saga of the family burial is one that truly happened but is hard to credit. When family members die, it is very important that many attend the burial and to be buried in one's ancestral home is highly desirable. Constance and others hired a taxi to take them to Qumbu each paying 200 Rand and with them went the body. All would have been well had the taxi not broken down and the eighteen year old driver had no solution to their problem. In the middle of the night another passing vehicle negotiated whatever money they could pool together to take them to the nearest point of their destination and they were all dropped off near Maclear. From here on they took turns in carrying the body over rough terrain, crossing streams in rain and mist and the plastic wrappings were becoming a bit problematic as was the condition of the body. "Oh, Medem, it was terrible and we were so pleased to get there in the end – the body it was not smelling good!" I have no idea what laws existed to permit a body to be moved in this way. Needless to say, upon their return the owner of the taxi was besieged by these angry passengers for a refund of their 200 Rand each – which they got.

As time passed, a serious setback occurred in Constance's health – she developed cancer of the colon. She was to have surgery at Groote Schuur Hospital but her husband would not sign the papers – it seemed that culturally they did not believe in cutting into a cancer. "Give me the ******! pen, doctor" I will sign the papers myself" said Constance. And so it was that Constance had the surgery. She had at least four Medems for whom she worked and we all visited her in the large ward and took her many things she would need. My heart skipped a beat when I saw her without her 'doek' for she was quite grey haired and I had never realised this strong little woman could be grey haired. She had to have a stoma and it was arranged that she would receive a monthly supply of bags. Once recovered, the doctor said to her that if she would drop some of her domestic work, he would arrange to get her a disability grant as from now on he considered her work too onerous. In order to obtain a disability grant one's earned income should not exceed a certain amount. Constance decided to keep me and Mrs. Griffiths to be her Medems.

She saw me through a time when my husband died suddenly, and I looked forward to her happy, smiling face when she arrived on my doorstep as I went through a period of loneliness.

A year or two later I retired and sold my large home for a smaller one and it was Constance who hauled packing boxes into my car – stoma and all – there was no curbing her strength and off we set for a new little home which delighted her as much as it did me. Far less work into the bargain and plenty of surplus things which I no longer needed found their way into her home in the Transkei.

The day came when her husband had reached retirement age and he arrived home with a cheque for 30,000 Rand in his pocket – a fortune never to be seen again. He was King of Langa for a night and heavy and riotous drinking took place and expansive tales of what he was going to do with all that money were shared with all around him. Constance watched and listened with great consternation and one wise old man agreed with Constance that it should be saved to buy cattle in the Transkei when they retired there. The night wore on and eventually the husband slept the deep sleep produced by the effects of too much alcohol. Constance removed the cheque from his pocket and was off to Claremont at the crack of dawn to visit a firm of attorneys with her Community of Property Marriage contract with her.

Having had a mission school education, Constance wrote and spoke well and was certainly no fool. She had learnt her rights from the Black Sash and knew that half of that money was legally hers. She handed it over to the attorneys to place in a Trust Account until the matter could be resolved with her husband.

For an African husband to be so confronted by his spouse was unthinkable and silent anger was his response. He then offered her a 1,000 Rand share but Constance stood her ground, explaining that it was for their mutual benefit that she wished to buy cattle in the Transkei. A stalemate existed for a great length of time until eventually he was compelled to sign the attorney's papers allowing Constance the half share of the payout.

It was with great sadness that I said goodbye to this strong, courageous woman. She had always admired a Royal Albert cup and saucer with violets on it which I had bought in a sale at Harrods in London and it was this that I presented to her to keep in her rondavel in the Transkei to remind her of all the cups of tea she had made for me. The doctor at Groote Schuur offered to give her a letter to the East London Hospital to collect her monthly supply of bags but she replied "Don't do me any favours, doctor, I want to come to Cape Town to visit my Medems!"

This, in due course, stopped and 20 years later I feel that she lies under the ground peacefully in Qumbu where she came from.

Val Christoffersen (SI Cape of Good Hope, South Africa)

Anita Raghu Belagodu *was born in Dharwar, Karnataka, India. Her younger days were spent on scenic beach shores of South Kanara. She now lives in Bangalore and has worked there for most of her life. She has done her post graduate in Clinical Psychology, has trained children in soft skills, been a school teacher and Career Counsellor. She is a special educator for dyslexic children and an accomplished creative writer. Anita has published her own book of poems and contributed poems to various anthologies and online journals. She has recited poems on All India Radio, won the Best Poet Award by Poets International and the Prize in Poetry in Motion Contest, USA. She has also participated on a Regional TV show on 'Examination Stress'. Anita has been President of SI Bangalore. She is happily married to Raghu Belagodu, a businessman, and they are blessed with two children – Rachna, a Marketing Consultant and Aditya, an undergraduate student of Civil Engineering.*

On Woman Empowerment

I am in love with this woman
Her secret, mysterious ways.
Her love and sacrifice defy a dozen deaths of unkind mankind.
She is for one, mightier than a man!

Seen a mistake in Christening her Weaker Sex.
A blunder in calling her Girl Child.
Female Foeticide! Not even dogs differentiate!
Yet, she dares and bares all to rebel an entire human race?

Deaf ears care less to hear her woes against Child Marriage.
Blind eyes fail to see burns victims or angry dowry deaths.
In ancient days, she dumbfounded people with Sati system
With resilience, overcomes domestic abuse with her winning ways.

Be it a stormy marriage or a gender-biased workplace,
Partial in-laws or impartial laws, both legal and illegal,
She will rise and rise like a PHOENIX
At every crisis, challenged!

Her androgynous instincts, last, live and endure to celebrate
An undying spirit of womanhood, carried through daughters.
She walks the world with pride and unparalled stride.
Creator's best – A Woman Empowered!

Anita R Belagodu (SI Bangalore, India)

How People Are

Twenty years old and cool. Too cool. Not terribly worldly-wise, thinking that people encountered were "just how people are" and taking them in my stride.

Then – oh joy! – an invitation to spend Easter weekend with my boyfriend's family. We had met as students, both of us away from home. This was an adventure beyond the local school-ish friendships and in a part of the English countryside that I did not know.

I arrived to a warm welcome into a close family whom I had never met before, only knowing from Simon, my boyfriend, that he had been brought up in India and his parents now lived in an apartment within a minor stately home.

The gathering of close siblings was obviously a joyous reunion of reminiscences and family jokes. All was going well.

We sat down to dinner and Mother presented a delicious and full plate before each of us. A moment's pause, then suddenly arms lunged across the table, forks stabbed at every plate, retrieving trophies of chosen food to their own plates.

I looked down. One sad little potato sat in a smear of gravy on my plate.

"This is what we do", whispered Simon. "Put your arms round your plate if you don't want to join in".

Too late.

I didn't know whether to laugh or cry but seemed to be largely unnoticed as everyone tucked in.

I ate slowly and learned fast.

I also learned that weekend that people are not always as they appear to be – as the family eccentricities emerged!

Father never took all his clothes off to bathe; one week his top half had a good wash and the second week he submerged his bottom half in the iron bath in the chill bathroom where the ancient pull-flush toilet reared menacingly in the corner, proud to have the legend 'The Thunderer' raised on the high cistern.

Mother's ruin consisted of a barrel of cider, never mentioned, at the foot of the parental bed and Mother withdrew from the family after these raucous meals to marinate gently in alcohol.

The ornamental poppies in the fabulous garden were dismissed as "disappointing" compared with the smoking opportunities of opium poppies in India.

Memories of the strange but comfortable domestic routine of this household remain with me; good-natured, grand but relaxed, oblivious to norms and rules but with a curiously pleasurable aspect which I enjoyed on many subsequent visits.

I stayed in touch with Simon for years and managed to escape marriage, inadvertently and shockingly casual, by arriving too late for our own wedding.

Families? There's nothing as odd as "how people are".

Pat Fergusson (SI The Fylde, England)

Ann Reeves *was born in London, but has lived all her life in Kent, England. She currently lives in a small village between Ashford and Folkestone – not far from the end of the Channel Tunnel. Ann has two children. She claims to have been a Soroptimist since she was in her late teens, when her mother joined SI Ashford and she helped her at a number of events. She sold raffle tickets, served coffee, took money at the door for special events – and is sure that, for a long time, it was not noticed that she was not officially a member! She did finally join in 1992 and since then was Club President in 2000-01 and Regional President for South East England in 2006-07. She is currently Regional Officer for Programme Action. As a retired teacher of technology, it comes as no surprise that Ann enjoys making things – including noticeboards, photo greetings cards, engraved glassware for special occasions and beaded necklaces.*

Jo Spencer *is a retired pharmacist, originally from Whitstable in Kent, England. She currently lives in a small village between Ashford and Folkestone – not far from the end of the Channel Tunnel. She has been a member of SI Ashford for many years. She has one daughter, Ann, to whom she told this story of the beginnings of her working life.*

Life with Bottles, Ampoules and Tablets

Dr Wilf Linnell was Head of Chemistry at the School of Pharmacy in Bloomsbury Square. We met and I was soon enrolled at the School (now University) known as the Square. I started a three year apprenticeship at the Metropolitan Hospital, Dalston, East London. It was 1937 and I was just 18 years old.

We made many of our own medicines by the gallon from raw materials. Our out-patients were mostly Jewish and we had a clinic where the doctor spoke Yiddish. I loved my three years there. At the same time I went to evening classes at Sir John Cass in Aldgate, four nights a week and studied Chemistry, Physics, Botany and Zoology. My future husband George was working there. His friend Bill taught Botany. After a while he and Bill used to come to my home in Whitstable for weekends and became family friends. I took the Cass exams at the end of my two years and failed miserably in Physics. It took me another year before I passed the pre-scientific test. This time I failed in Botany, which was actually my best subject! I had left that to look after itself while concentrating on the subjects I found so much more difficult.

When war broke out in 1939 I stayed at home with Mother while I re-sat my Botany; my father's city office was evacuated to Wokingham and George was called up as he had been in the army before. He was immediately sent to Arras in France, with the Intelligence Service. The war hotted up and the Germans came through Northern France towards Arras. George's unit packed and went to the coast, unfortunately while George was out in the town. He got back to find they had left without him, so he went out and found an empty truck with a driver. George said "What are you doing?"

"Waiting for orders" was the response.

"Right," said George. "You've got them!"

With that the two of them set off for the coast, picking up stragglers on the way. Luckily they went to Boulogne rather than Dunkirk so didn't get stranded on the beaches. While they were waiting to leave they sheltered from an air-raid under some railway carriages they were meant to be guarding. When the raid had passed they crawled out from under the sheltering carriage, and realised only at that point that they held ammunition!!! George managed to get on the last boat to leave Boulogne harbour as the German tanks rolled down the hill towards them, having dumped the lorry and its contents into the harbour as they left so that the Germans were denied its use. He disembarked at Folkestone and made his way to Whitstable and our house. It was a lovely hot summer and we watched the dog fights overhead, with George and my mother racing to be first to the best viewing windows. He was given leave on his return from France. They didn't seem to know quite what to do with him and kept extending his leave, so he was able to spend a considerable period of time with us. He was eventually sent to Winchester and from there to Jerusalem to be in charge of medical stores. At least he was safe there!

In September 1941 I went to Cardiff, where the School of Pharmacy had been evacuated. They had managed to get lab space and lecture rooms at Cardiff University. I had wonderful digs in Whitchurch and made lifelong friends. They even provided a camp bed in the sitting room for George when he was on leave. The bombing in Cardiff was mostly in the docks and we were lucky in

Whitchurch, but on one occasion after a raid a friend said "Let's go and have a look at the town." We walked down Queen Street and only discovered later that there were unexploded bombs there!

George was demobbed, got a job in London and we were married in 1942. It was also the year in which I got my degree and the Square moved back to Bloomsbury. I was made a Demonstrator in Dispensing, the lowest of the low! I fire-watched on top of the building, we were lucky and there were no fire bombs. Then the Buzz bombs started. We used to dash for the basement's narrow winding stairs which we felt were the safest. My childhood friend Patsy and I had found a small, one room basement flat in Pimlico, safe unless the bombers went for Victoria station!

I stayed at the Square for a year, then went to the West Middlesex Hospital where I saw the start of the use of penicillin. It was so scarce that we had to send our porter to Hyde Park to pick up enough treatment for one patient.

After 18 months I was appointed Head Pharmacist at the Elizabeth Garret Anderson Hospital (now the UNITE building on the Euston Road) which was an all-women institution – staff and patients.

The dispensary had a large main room with a big bench in the middle, having drawers and cupboards to contain small packets and containers of ampoules and tablets with a desk at one end. Round the sides of the room were shelves of bulk ingredients, ointments …and the all-important outpatient hatch. At the end there was a small sterilising room where we made intravenous solutions. We had an old-fashioned autoclave, sintered glass filter, oven and sink. The long side of the dispensary had large sash windows and two sinks. These were wooden, so that bottles did not break, but it was necessary to leave the tap gently dripping at the weekend so that the wood did not shrink and leak.

Outside the dispensary door to the left was an external door to a very large yard. On the side of this was a wide opening with large gates leading to the Euston Road. To the right of the dispensary door were three to four steps up to the main corridor, the lift and stairs up to the wards and along to the secretaries and typists' office and the lovely main hall and front door. To the right of the dispensary lifts and stairs the corridor continued parallel to the outpatient reception office, outpatients and on to the Path. Lab.

The first job in the mornings was refilling the ward baskets. I think there were 130 or so beds! When the outpatients came through to our hatch one of us would work there while the others proceeded with the baskets and then made ointments (in pounds) mixtures in Winchesters (four pints) suppositories and pessaries by the dozen! Much more interesting than modern pharmacy.

I was there for a couple of years before the National Health Service came. We were a voluntary hospital relying on contributions for finance, so we had to be as economical as possible. I had to report once a month on our expenditure to the house committee – Lady Vesty, the Honourable Mrs Mulholland (lady in waiting to the Queen), Mrs Gilmour and the Secretary. There was a recovery home at the Rosa Morrison House in Barnet. An annual garden party and sale was held there. I used to make hand cream, in very short supply in those days (with permission) which sold very well and was in demand. I can say it was used in the Royal Household as Mrs Mulholland used to bring me her empty jars to refill!

The staff in the dispensary were a very happy group. I continued to work there until a month before the birth of my daughter in 1954.

I was a Pharmacist for the rest of my working life but I will always have particularly good memories of those early days of my career.

Jo Spencer as told to her daughter *Ann Reeves (SI Ashford, England)*

Toward the Unknown Region

And so the son,
whom I have made
and unmade,
nurtured
yet so maimed,
sets out
towards the unknown region,
where snow shuffles shaggily seaward,
scalpels of blue-green ice sculpt and sear,
and cold burns bodies black;
sheltered by a mere membrane,
a frame of friendship.
Who will return?

Written when my disabled son went with a university mountaineering expedition to Greenland

Clare Harding (SI Blackburn, England)

Rema Ramchandran *was born in Chennai, India. She has lived for most of her life, however, in Mumbai, the commercial capital of India. Rema has been a banker for most of her professional life with the UK based Standard Chartered Bank. She currently lives in Bangalore and has been a Soroptimist for the last nine years, since almost the inception of SI Bangalore. She has been a Past President of the Club and now holds the post of Media Officer for the National Association of Soroptimists of India. Rema is married to Ramchandran (Raja) and they have two children, both of whom are married. She enjoys reading, writing and interacting with people.*

Something I Would Like To Share

I am a Soroptimist from Bangalore, India. I am a wife and mother of two children who are grown-up. This incident which I want to narrate will stay in my mind forever and I feel reflects the power of prayer.

My son Varun, a handsome young lad of 23 years, was pursuing his Management Studies in a neighbouring city called Mysore. He was residing in the college hostel. It was Sunday morning. It was a matter of routine that every Sunday I would call Varun and exchange all the news. I called as usual receiving no response from his phone. It was 10.30am. I thought to myself perhaps he had a late night and was still asleep. I called again after an hour to receive no response again. I started to get concerned and called my husband who was travelling back home from another city (Chennai). I requested he try and contact Varun from his phone. He called back saying there was no response.

It was 1pm and I had invited guests to join me for lunch. As we sat down to eat I got a call from my son. In a feeble voice I could hardly recognise he told me one of his friends, incidentally bearing the same name Varun, had met with a serious accident and was hospitalised. My heart sank and I asked my son if he was hurt. He answered hesitantly that he was all right. Call it a mother's sixth sense or intuitive ability, I sensed something was amiss.

I called my son Varun later and enquired about the actual details. He told me his friend Varun was riding the bike with my son on the pillion seat. Being

Saturday night they dined out and were returning to the hostel. There was no power that night as the street lights had gone out and in the dark their bike hit a stationary truck. When the truck moved off my son's friend was dragged along with the vehicle and his head struck the pavement. He went into a coma and never recovered.

My heart missed a beat as he narrated the tragedy. Then, he said "Ma, I don't know what happened to me. I felt I was lifted from the bike seat by some unseen hand and placed on the pavement. I could walk around. I have just a few scratches on my leg. I am absolutely fine."

This was very strange as I knew that normally the pillion rider comes off worse in an accident. I remembered the moment I called him. I recall I had started praying thinking something untoward had occurred.

This incident will always remain in my mind, one which I can never forget. At times I agonise, I re-live the times I visited the hospital to see my son's friend battling for his life. My heart goes out to the parents of my son's friend and his family. Their son didn't survive and was declared brain dead. I thank God for his mercy in saving my son.

Rema Ramchandran (Si Bangalore, India)

Kate Sergeant *was born in Bromley, Kent, England. She was brought up in Staffordshire, read Medieval Archaeology at University College London and pursued her first career in advertising, becoming International Media Manager at Saatchi and Saatchi in 1989. Kate moved to Tunbridge Wells in 1995 to work for Kimberly-Clark and became a Soroptimist in 2007. Never one to do things by halves, Kate launched straight into the Glasgow International Conference in 2007 and served as Programme Action Officer for SI Tunbridge Wells and District 2008-10. Since 2010 Kate has been working for the Kent and Medway Alzheimer's Society as Support Services Manager, following the diagnosis of both of her parents with Alzheimer's in 2008. Kate enjoys running, swimming, horse riding, improvisational theatre, community singing and samba drumming when she is not jumping out of aeroplanes!*

Jumping for John

It was a very exciting day that I will never forget. There were ten of us skydiving from Headcorn Airport to fundraise for the Alzheimer's Society Tesco partnership and we all landed safe and sound! I was jumping in memory of my father who died from Alzheimer's in 2010 and had served with the Royal Artillery Parachute Regiment during his National Service.

We were briefed first thing and had to wait around for the low cloud to clear. Then everything happened very quickly. We were put into jumpsuits (with handles on the arms and legs!) parachute harness, soft helmet, gloves and goggles, then quickly bundled onto a little plane which we entered via a step ladder. We all sat on the floor of the plane, crammed on top of each other. I was firmly strapped to my instructor, Richard, who is also a local farrier – so we talked horses on the way up.

When the side door opened at 12,000 feet I felt incredibly excited and unexpectedly calm. The ground far below was a tiny patchwork of misty brown and green fields. I felt a very strong connection with Dad at this point, knowing that he had experienced the same thing so many times before me. I felt safe and purposeful and really wanted to jump. We bottom-shuffled forward to the open door and hung our legs over the side. The force of the wind was absolutely phenomenal and the air was very cold. I held tight onto the handles on my jumpsuit with my arms crossed.

Richard pushed us off and we were out. The fast cold air hit me like an all over body brick. I arched myself backwards and prepared to scream, as we had been briefed, but nothing came out… just like a strange dream. I began to realise that I should at least try to breathe, even at 120 mph, and did manage a few short breaths before I felt the lift of the harness as the red and white parachute opened up above us. My ears had popped so I had to clear them by pinching my nose and blowing.

Flying the parachute was the most beautiful and fun experience. The fields had got quite a lot bigger by now and I could clearly see the local reservoir, Bewl Water, twinkling below us. Richard handed me the steering straps and we banked and wheeled our way downwards like giddy children, laughing and whooping all the way. I could have stayed up there all day.

Eventually it was time to land, saying hello to the sheep and newborn lambs as we passed, and Richard steered us down. I held my legs out in front of me by the handles on my jumpsuit and landed, ever so slightly inelegantly, on one foot and one knee. Brightly coloured parachutes were billowing on the ground all around us and we were all wearing the hugest grins you have ever seen!!

Kate Sergeant (SI Tunbridge Wells, England)

The following poems share tales of those often forgotten women in today's society – the disabled, the elderly and the struggling artist.

Disabled Woman's Voice

I am a proud disabled woman.
My body and mind may challenge me.

I have learned my own special way
To meet my needs, to deal with life.

I have dreams, and I have goals.
And you will see, I will achieve.

Give me respect, as I deserve.
I will persevere for my rights.

Disabled friends, they understand.
We share fears, joys, and support.

I am female with feelings as you.
Include me, enable me, celebrate me.

I am a disabled woman, very much alive.
Hear me, care about me, treasure me!

Lois Herman (SI Greater Minneapolis, Minnesota, USA)

Older Woman's Voice

I am an older, elderly, woman.
The lines on my face are etched with the seasons of my life.

I am not pretty anymore. My hair is grey, my skin sagging,
In a world fixated on youth and beauty.

I am frailer now, more fragile, more often ill.
I cannot afford all the medical care I need.

I want to tell my children stories of my life
But they are busy, not so interested in my legacy.

I am lonely. My husband, also old, has dementia.
I feel isolated, ignored, forgotten.

What has happened to the respect for elders,
To the valuing of life from cradle to grave?

Where is social justice to care for old women
And provide for their special needs and rights?

I am an older woman, but I am very much alive.
Hear me, care about me, help me, treasure me.

Lois Herman (SI Greater Minneapolis, Minnesota, USA)

Margaret Sharon Olscamp *lives near Bathurst, New Brunswick, Canada where she was born. She is a volunteer with the AMDHHA, an Acadian-Irish historic property holding and a bilingual non-profit organisation in Bathurst. Her dearest hope is to have many kindred spirits join her to help develop a cultural/ community centre at the Maison Doucet-Hennessy House which is the focus of AMDHHA. Here she recently opened a small art studio where she paints. Sharon is an amateur Bodhran player and her free spirit encouraged her to take up violin a year ago. She and her musician husband Gilles are blessed with two children and three grandchildren. Sharon is 'a friend' of Soroptimism and was introduced to Soroptimist International through the 'Join me on the Bridge' campaign, as advertised on the website. Unable to attend any meetings due to the lack of clubs near her, she subscribes to the newsletter through email.*

Job Equity

A writer...
An artist...
Often...
Not always the woman...
But often
The person
Faceless
Voice
Yearning
To speak is to breathe
So desperate
So cold
Hearken the Stone Rejected
Rise from the pillow
And work... And wonder... Why?

Why some get paid
Some...

Margaret Sharon Olscamp (SI Friend, Dunlop, New Brunswick, Canada)

The Godmother

Mrs Eastham likes her weekly routine. Ann calls on Monday for Mrs Eastham's shopping list, returning on Tuesday with her weekly needs, weaving around the hairdresser, each as regular as clockwork. Wednesdays are just as busy with Jim, the Church Visitor, the girl who does the laundry, the cleaner, and then Thursday is Mrs Eastham's day for a manicure, followed by a leisurely afternoon watching David, the gardener, tend the lawns and tidy the flower beds. Friday, the milkman is to be paid and the fishmonger calls, then final preparations for the weekend with sweets in little dishes for Sunday visitors, piles of photos and albums still needing a little attention and occasionally a delivery or cold-caller, quite unnecessary and intrusive in such a busy routine.

Mrs Eastham likes the weekly routine; the way her visitors contribute to the smooth passage of time and the efficiency of a house well-run. Her home is everything and as Mrs Eastham, now 100 years old, no longer goes out, this is where she wants to remain until the end of her days.

Orphaned at two years old, Mrs Eastham – Connie – and her sister, May, were raised in children's homes and sometimes stayed with their grandmother. They had a peripatetic routine, criss-crossing the North of England and eventually settling into work which, for Connie, developed into being a College Bursar, marriage to Frank and one son, John, who died in infancy. Her husband had been Mayor; she the Mayoress and Connie's celebrations for her 100th birthday brought together recollections and faces from her long years of service.

Her sister, May's life took a similar path and when the sisters married, they vowed to each other never, ever to rely on 'welfare' again and to stay forever as mistresses of their own homes.

Connie was widowed 55 years ago and lived next door to her sister, also widowed, both fiercely independent and refusing to either live together or to be cared for, keen volunteers and supporters of their respective churches and their local community.

May died in 2009 and everyone who knew Connie anticipated that "she'll go in no time" but Connie decreed "business as usual", missing her sister enormously but with the grit and determination to keep going.

In her life she had experienced two World Wars, huge developments in communications, technology and travel, remembering events with clarity and detail. With poor hearing and eyesight, Connie's home remains unchanged for decades and in her mind's eye, she remains "the Lady of the House", receiving visitors and enjoying her independence in spite of so many friends now having died and with almost no family.

This is a true story from Connie's point of view but the reality is a different version.

When May died it became apparent that neither sister had been managing their affairs but propped each other up, covering long ignored domestic and personal affairs and generally unwilling to look realistically at their situation. Why would you? Realism becomes blurred as extreme old age approaches and sight diminishes, enabling rose-tinted spectacles to be a pleasing option.

Diminutive and exceedingly frail, Connie is nevertheless sharp and aware. However, her frailty necessitates carers to help with every aspect of her life, calling four times a day, whilst Connie's goddaughter and her husband plumbed Connie's bottomless handbag filing system, unravelling years of ignored affairs and gradually sorting it all out.

Maybe it is the image in Connie's head of remaining "the Lady of the House", endorsed by blindness and deafness that keeps her going. She tells visitors that she has seen the fish man and bought some nice fillet for dinner, but has she? I'm sure it doesn't matter but it is interesting to witness such a tiny and determined woman staying true to the promise she made with her sister over 70 years ago; that independence would be preciously guarded at all costs.

She falls; medics arrive and she refuses to go to hospital. "Patient flatly refused to go to Accident and Emergency", read the paramedic's report. Her body is failing, her organs and functions becoming unreliable, yet Connie manages to blank these inconveniences. It seems likely that if she acknowledges her physical decline, her independence will be curtailed. She is amused by the cat-and-mouse aspects of her relationship with support services and she is irritated by sentimentality and the notion that she is old and helpless. But she does like to be called, "Mrs Eastham; just so people know I'm married and they don't get any ideas".

For every person who comes into contact with Mrs Eastham and says that she really should be looked after full time, to stop being heroic and retreat to a care home, there are just as many who recognise her strength, her ability and her right to make her own decisions.

"I need to keep my mind busy," she says, snapping off the radio and reciting the alphabet back-to-front. What a lesson for us all and how enriching to have a friend such as Mrs Eastham.

Pat Fergusson (SI The Fylde, England)

Breaking the Rules

It isn't done to gossip,
or sunbathe in the nude;
To eat food with one's fingers
is looked upon as rude;
and if to our appointments
we're 30 minutes late,
we won't say sorry when we're not –
it does them good to wait!

All shibboleths and taboos
which used to rule our lives,
we'll break to gain the freedom
for which each woman strives.
So if we want to skinny-dip
or drink more than we should,
we're growing old disgracefully,
and doesn't it feel good!

Joan Lees (SI Waimea, New Zealand)

Going for a Century

It is 1998. Here I am running a residential home for the elderly and loving the challenge.

It is carnival time in our small town. "What" you may well ask, "has that got to do with an old people's home?" A lot, I can assure you, as I will tell you the tale of 'Going for a Century'.

We are a community of 33 residents of both genders, ages ranging from 76 to 93 years. Each and every one of the residents are real characters in their own way which ensures that life is never boring working there as every day throws up something different.

There is Taff who sits in a chair facing the front door. He orders all the visitors about as they come visiting, then rushes into my office to tell me who has come in and who they are visiting. He always has a cigarette in his mouth, which uses up his entire pension. I have a nasty suspicion he coerces a few "fags" as he calls them out of our visitors when his money has run out which is five days into the week. Will also sits in the hallway coughing well as he chain smokes daily. "The war didn't kill me" he says, "and neither will these, I'll go when I'm ready". As he is our 93 year old who are we to tell him what to do? I could go through them all describing their little idiosyncrasies but to the carnival we must go.

Old age can be very boring and tedious. The staff works well as a team, always trying to think of ways to keep our residents interested in life. Why not take them to the carnival, not as spectators, I mused, but as participants. What will they say when the idea is put to them? Getting together the staff and residents we had a meeting to discuss the idea. The residents on the whole thought it would be fun but what did it all entail? Had we overreached ourselves I was thinking, a thought somewhat reinforced when Will said, "Leave me out of this, I'm too old for such things, don't forget I'm going to be 100 years old before too long." That did it.

"Going for a century" one of the staff yelled, "that's it. Good old Will, a birthday party float with you cutting the cake". Will harrumphed but a small smile played around his mouth – though he said nothing. We all discussed the idea for a little longer with the residents becoming really interested and excited. "What do we do? Do we have to talk? What do we wear?" and so on. It was decided that once the skeleton of the idea had been filled out everyone would be given a job to do. Fortunately many of the staff had husbands who were willing to help us out. One was a farmer who said he would loan us a tractor and trailer and would also drive the float, another husband who was artistic said he would make a huge cardboard birthday cake and paint it appropriately. My job was to book us in for the procession and organise work periods where we all got stuck into making decorations and a huge banner to hang on both sides of the float saying "GOING FOR A CENTURY". What fun we all had, quite a few daily tasks did not get done but everyone was happy and who cared if the beds weren't made until late afternoon or dinner was 15 minutes late, or the bath water went cold as we forgot about it being so engrossed in our handiwork. Everything was going along swimmingly, all the details with the organisers had been sorted out, decorations made and the residents were looking forward to partaking in something very different from the normal daily routine.

Then the hierarchy struck.

"Oh no, oh dear no, whatever next" and so on and so on, they said. A visit from the Deputy Head of Social Services nearly put a stop to our little adventure. I was informed it was an impossible idea and that health and safety would on no account allow old people to be sitting around a huge cardboard cake on a moving vehicle. Everyone was very disappointed so another joint meeting was held on how we could get round this problem. Every problem has a solution, therefore it no longer is a problem I was once told. With this in mind we had a brainstorming session and once more someone had a brainwave. "Let us dress the staff up as old people on the float and get the daughters of staff to push the residents in wheelchairs alongside the float". They can be waving Union Jacks or musical instruments – whatever they wish. Some of them could carry decorated buckets on their laps to catch the money people throw at their favourite float". Discussing this with the residents, they agreed it was a good idea and thankfully the hierarchy agreed too. What a relief, as by this time everyone, staff and residents alike, wanted to join in the festivities with a carnival float. The day arrived and we were ready.

Imagine my total amazement when the young girls turned up ready for their wheelchair push all dressed up as can-can dancers. The mothers of these girls had kept this a tight secret from me but they looked fantastic and really set the atmosphere for a carnival. The residents who had known about this thought it was a huge joke on me – which indeed it was! All set now and off we went to get into position on the Green ready to join the float parade as it went around the town. The residents all began to wave their flags, blow their whistles, bang their tambourines – raring to go. The staff at the 'birthday party' played their parts with great gusto and even had little fisticuffs over the last drop of whisky in the bottle. Spittle flew everywhere when they playacted blowing the make-believe candles out causing much laughter from both residents and the crowd standing watching the whole scene. The can-can girls gave plenty of 'high-kicks' which pleased many of the spectators, turning the whole task of pushing wheelchairs into fun. The buckets filled up with coins at an amazing rate and to crown a really happy day we won 2ⁿᵈ prize!

Who says you can't do things when you're old?

Mary McCormick (SI Lancaster, England)

Letting Go

In fancy I shrug on my pack,
walk into the wilderness of the past,
feel of wind in my hair again, the sound
of brawling creeks, bellbirds' song.
I camp under the stars,
the smell of woodsmoke, a morepork's call,
wake to fresh sunny mornings
or rain drumming on tent roofs.
Once I lived for my games –
contests of skill and endurance
challenged every thought: each muscle.
Now I must make do with mental pastimes:
crosswords, Scrabble, quizzes and my pen.

Joan Lees (SI Waimea, New Zealand)

No Title Necessary

I knew you were dead
when the notices stopped
in the newspaper
I knew you were dead
when I had to take my car
for a service
I knew you were dead
when I had to change
the light bulbs
I knew you were dead
when I had to manage
the family finances
I knew you were dead
when there were no anniversary presents
no one put petrol in my car
no one kissed me goodbye
phoned me everyday at twelve
brought home the evening paper
made the morning tea
hugged me on the stairs
made me laugh every day
discussed our children
loved Sulka ties
weekends at Rawdons
biscuits and chocolates
French Burgundy's
Beef Wellington
Spanish omelettes
Brussel sprouts
early walks
late nights
London
Dancing
Trains

Travel
Me

Hannah Lurie (SI Durban, South Africa)

Voices from the Past

Ignore whispers from long ago, winds
of blame through mind and spirit.
'If only' brings depression,
shame and remorse.
Look into the past, believe
that those days are over. Learn
from our ancient mistakes, but
leave them buried in oblivion,
and step forward into today's world.
Life is for living. Take ownership
of the future, without
the impediment of those
voices from the past.

Joan Lees (SI Waimea, New Zealand)

TALES OF SOROPTIMISM

Promila Khandelwal *was born and brought up in Calcutta (now Kolkata), West Bengal, India. Born in a liberal and educated family, she completed her MA and B.Ed., trained in several arts and crafts, got married and had two sons. She started her teaching career when her children were of school age. In 1982 she moved to Burdwan due to her husband's profession. In 1992, she joined SI Burdwan and then the change came. This was the first experience of sisterhood for her. Promila has been an active Soroptimist since 1994. She has served as Club Programme Action Officer, Club President and Club Rep from 1994-2000. She was elected as P&P Chairperson of the National Association of Soroptimist International of India (NASI) from 2000-02, Vice President of NASI of INDIA 2002-04, President Elect of NASI of INDIA 2004-06, President of NASI OF INDIA 2006-08, Councillor for NASI of INDIA in SIGBI 2007-09. She attended the Cardiff Conference of SIGBI in 2009. For the last two years Promila is the Link Co-ordinator for SI Burdwan.*

Elder Sister

I joined SI Burdwan in August 1992 and suddenly I found myself in a different world. The fellowship we enjoy transforms acquaintances to friends and friends to life-long sisterhood.

In 1992, I was very new to Soroptimism. I had to go to Calcutta to meet the then SIGBI President. I was worried where I would spend the night – for Calcutta is far from Burdwan and after dinner it would not be possible to return. Then one of the senior Soroptimist members of SI Calcutta offered me the opportunity to stay the night with her. We had never met in person, but when I went to the meeting place, a member came forward and introduced herself. "I am Chitra di" – di means 'elder sister'. How relieved I was when I heard this. With these words we were no longer strangers.

After so many years as a Soroptimist, I found out that Soroptimism is a wonderful journey towards friendship. It unites us in our common path – in one's joys and in one's sorrows.

This spirit makes us enjoy internationality and universalism.

Once a Soroptimist, always a Soroptimist!

Promila Khandelwal (SI Burdwan, India)

Chris Knight *lives at Deception Bay, Queensland, Australia. She has been married to Graeme for 23 years. She enjoys travel, fishing, reading and playing Lawn Bowls. Professionally, Chris works for the Queensland State Government as a Senior Advisor and Internal Auditor. She is an avid SI Chatliner and has been a member of Soroptimist International for 27 years. Her passion for social justice, empowering women and participating in community development activities has enabled her to facilitate workshops at Federation Conferences and International Conventions. Chris has held a variety of offices at Club, Region, Federation and International levels. She was SISWP Federation Liaison Officer for Project Sierra. Chris transferred her membership to SI Pine Rivers (now SI Moreton North) after the dissolution of the Brisbane City Club. Chris is also a writer and has contributed articles to Soroptimist magazines and local community radio/ media on topics relating to human rights, including violence against women and human trafficking. In 2008, Chris received the Australia Day Award for Citizen of the Year in recognition of her Soroptimist contributions to the local and global community. Chris regards herself as an earnest 'Little Hobbit' who tries to make a difference where she can!*

My Journey

I was born in a little country town called Bright in Australia. When I was very young, I became a ward of the state and along with my younger brother was put up for adoption. While I have no memory of any neglect or abuse, I do bare a scar on my right arm from what was apparently a cigarette burn. We moved several times, changing schools, and in the middle of my secondary education we shifted to a remote mining community in far North Queensland. At 14, I began working full time and finished my Junior Certificate by correspondence. My parents were hard workers and always believed in sharing whatever they had. I grew up on the philosophy that everyone deserves a 'fair go' and you need to 'pay your own way' and be always ready to 'lend a hand'.

When I was 18, I left home, fell in love (or so I thought) and worked in construction and mining camps. This was probably one of the loneliest and saddest times of my life. I was isolated, had little contact with the outside world with no female friends or extended family close by. It took several years before I realised that living with a partner who was abusive, who gambled most of our savings and who drank a lot was not how I wanted to spend the rest of my life. So after a very sad separation, I got a cat, a full-time job, a car and met my husband Graeme. At 26 I was invited to become a Charter Member of a local Soroptimist International Club and suddenly I had hundreds of big sisters, aunties and grandmothers. They encouraged me, hugged me and shared their life experiences and wisdom. We worked on lots of local projects. I would go off to the Region Meetings and ask endless questions trying to understand more about this organisation. The turning point came after attending the SISWP Conference in 1988 and watching the video of the SI International Project *Bringing Safe Water for Senegal* (1985-89). It was then that I started to realise just what the word *International* in our name actually meant. I was so excited to know that women just like me were all around the world and cared enough to help our Soroptimist Sisters to provide safe drinking water to villages in Africa. There was Immediate Past President Betty Loughhead Turland (New Zealand) dancing around with the local villagers having a great time and Soroptimist International President Sadun Katipoglu (Turkey) who spoke about the work of Soroptimist International. Her passion for Soroptimist International touched a special place in my heart that created a dream that maybe one day I might be able to travel to Africa and do something special like Betty did.

Over the years this little dream lay dormant while I learnt more about SI by taking on positions at Club, Region, Federation and International level. One of my very special memories (and there have been many since) was back in 1999, when I had my first little 'Hobbit' experience. Just like Bilbo Baggins, I left the safe borders of 'The Shire' and ran off (actually I flew) overseas by myself to the SI Convention in Helsinki, Finland. What really enticed me to go to Finland was the overwhelming encouragement from the SI Chatliners and to my 'Cyber Godmother', Kate Moore, who enabled so many SI members around the world to get to know each other through the medium of email. Many of us back then did not know how to send an attachment or knew what a virus was until we got one! Together we shared ideas and many became life-long friends. Over the years 'The Hobbit' journeys have continued. In 2007, I was appointed the SISWP International Liaison for *Project Sierra* (2007-11) and worked closely with another special SI Chatliner friend Alison Sutherland who was the International Liaison for this project. In 2010, I turned 50 and was able to represent SISWP on the study tour to Sierra Leone where we visited many remote villages and talked to the local women and girls whom we were helping. I returned to Australia and became involved with my Club Members Audrey Martin and Caryl Ryan in supporting the women from Sierra Leone who had migrated to Australia as refugees – another amazing experience. In 2012, I was off on another little 'Hobbit' adventure with my good friend, travelling companion and SI Chatliner Sheilah Downs (who lives in Middle Earth New Zealand). After the SISWP Conference we had the pleasure of staying in Christchurch with PIP Betty Loughhead Turland and I got to hold a pot that Betty brought back with her from her visit to Senegal in 1985. I shared my story with Betty about how she inspired me – we are both planning to be in Istanbul in 2015 where Betty's International Presidency began.

How blessed and grateful I am to have been invited to join this amazing organisation all those years ago! I could never have imagined that my walking tracks would have taken me all around the world! To my Soroptimist Sisters whom I have stayed with and shared so many happy times together – thank you. To the International Presidents whom I have got to know – thank you for your leadership and friendship. My life has been greatly enriched.

Namaste.

Chris Knight (SI Moreton North, Australia)

Marja Reunis-de Rechter *was born in St. Jansteen, Zeeland, the Netherlands. She studied physiotherapy and manual therapy and now owns her own private practice. She has lived in Poland, Indonesia and Italy and is now living in Belgium. She became a Soroptimist in 1999 in Poland and is presently a member of the Soroptimist Club Roosendaal 'De Drie Rozen' (the Three Roses) in the Netherlands. Marja was the club's secretary in 2008-09 and she is now Assistant Programme Director for the South of the Netherlands. She is married to Ronald and has four children. She enjoys reading and acts in amateur theatre productions.*

How I Became a Soroptimist

It was May 1996 when we, my husband Ronald, my daughter Elke (five), my son Tom (three) and I left the Netherlands due to my husband's work for Philips. We went to Poland. Philips started a joint venture with the Polam factory in Bielsko-Biala, in the South of Poland. I gave up my Physiotherapy private practice in Roosendaal. Saying goodbye to our friends, family and home was the hardest part. The initial period in Poland was difficult: there were no expats, no international schools, not even a telephone line at our house. To start with, the contact with the Polish people was cold, yet we had great neighbours which made a big difference. The children quickly found their place and I soon started working on a voluntary basis as a physiotherapist with handicapped people in a day care centre. Learning the Polish language was a challenge, yet vital to be able to communicate. In 1997 Ruud was born in the local hospital, hospital number 1, in Bielsko-Biala. By this time we all felt at home in Poland, having formed many sincere friendships.

My friend Hanna, a member of the Soroptimist International club Bielko-Biala, asked me to teach the club the Dutch National anthem, as the SI club of Apeldoorn from the Netherlands was coming to visit and they wanted to surprise them! The contact with the Soroptimists was very warm and they asked me to join the club. I became a member in March 1999. I enjoyed the meetings and organising the fundraising events and projects. At the end of January 2000, however, we had to say goodbye because we were about to move to Belgium for half a year to prepare us for the subsequent move to Indonesia. In March, Anne was born and we enjoyed the time, being so close to our family in the Netherlands. In August we left for Indonesia, a completely different country: warm, welcoming people but people whose hearts are not as easily reached or thoughts understood. Here the children went to the International School and there was an expats' society. Soon I found my way by helping to organize the PTA (Parent/Teacher Association) at the Surabaya International School. I also became a member of the Tulip, a Dutch association that supports local schools in the kampong with projects such as renovations or building toilets and organises other important activities such as helping to fund cleft lip and palate operations. Again I learned to speak the language.

After 9/11, things changed: Indonesia was the biggest Muslim country and we were suddenly forced to act 'low profile'. There were lots of security measures, evacuation plans and a general state of uncertainty.

In 2002, Afghanistan was invaded and in October the Bali bombing happened. Bali was our safe haven due to the Hindu religion there, so the shock was immense. Now the government could no longer deny that there was terrorism in Indonesia and they started to support the expats more. It was a difficult period yet nothing negative happened to us personally.

At the end of 2003 we left for Italy – back to Europe. Italy was great but again you had to invest in the culture, the language, the huge history. All our children went to the International School of Turin and I became very actively involved in the PTA once again.

In 2006, after almost 11 years abroad, we came "back home", living just outside the Netherlands in Belgium. We had to re-integrate, which was sometimes more difficult than it had been to integrate into a whole new culture because it made you feel like a stranger in your own country.

In 2007 I renewed my membership with Soroptimist International with the club of Roosendaal Drie Rozen and I started my work again as a Physiotherapist. I also started as coordinator for the Dutch Union of Soroptimist Clubs to highlight programme work and international awareness. My extensive travels have taught me that it is important.

My belief is to focus on what we have in common, not on the differences, and to be realistic in our expectations. We should choose to encourage rather than to criticise and not be too quick to make judgements.

Sharing is caring.

Marja Reunis-de Rechter (SI Roosendaal Drie Rozen, The Netherlands)

Susan Joyce *was born in Albany, California, USA. Now retired, she previously owned and operated Joyce Printing, a large format printing and bindery company for 33 years. Susan is currently a resident of Lincoln, California. She is the mother of two sons and has five grandchildren. Susan joined Soroptimist International in 1972 and is presently a life member of SI Dixon, California. Susan has served in various Soroptimist positions, including Club President, on the region level as Founder Region Growth and Development Chair, Secretary, Director and Governor. Susan has served on the SIA Federation level as Growth and Development Chair and has helped to charter over 25 Soroptimist clubs. She has given numerous seminars regarding membership within her region, other SIA regions and at SIA Federation conventions. Susan loves to write poetry and short stories. She is also a soprano, has given numerous gospel concerts in churches and prisons and currently performs regularly in shows in her community.*

Violet Richardson Ward
(Founding President of Soroptimist International)

When I was Vice President of Soroptimist International of Richmond in 1975 I was solely responsible for planning the programme meetings for the club and obtaining interesting speakers. Because Violet Richardson Ward lived in a neighbouring city, I had the opportunity and pleasure of meeting Violet personally. To me she was Soroptimist royalty and she was also a very formidable presence.

When I joined the Soroptimists in 1972 the Richmond club was very conscious of orienting and educating all new members on all aspects of Soroptimism, and so of course that included the history of Violet as our Founding President and her influence on Soroptimism becoming an international organisation.

Violet was a very busy woman and I knew I would have to schedule her time well in advance of the meeting date. I telephoned Violet and she graciously accepted the invitation to speak and supplied a date. She asked what she should speak about and I told her we would be interested in knowing more about her as well as anything she'd like to share with us, and that it would be an honour to have her come.

Violet was 86 years old at the time. Considering her elderly, I asked if I could come and get her and drive her to the meeting. She told me that would not be necessary, that she still drove her car. I then asked her if she needed directions to the meeting place and she told me she knew exactly where it was. Our meeting place was the Richmond YWCA building. There were two flights of fairly steep stairs to the meeting room and no elevator was available. Though I didn't feel comfortable mentioning the stairs to her after her previous responses above, I was very concerned about her navigating the stairs.

When Violet arrived that day, I offered to give her my arm while ascending the stairs. She told me in no uncertain terms that she was not dead yet and immediately walked right past me with a very determined look on her face, ascending the stairs with speed and grace in front of me, leaving me breathless! At that point I was pretty embarrassed to say the very least.

That day Violet totally amused, entertained and kept her audience rapt in attention. Her presentation was powerful and included her personal family history, her travels, the formation of Soroptimism and her personal views. The meeting ran overtime and no one cared. We were all aware that Violet was a very unique woman with a very unique personal history.

Personally for me that day, Violet radiated extreme dignity softened by humility, extreme intellect, an extreme creative spirit and an extreme wealth of experience without any hint of self-importance. I realise I used the word 'extreme' numerous times in the previous sentence. Yes… Violet was an extreme person in all ways! She spoke her mind freely and got her opinions across with a great deal of finesse and humour. She was a woman who knew who she was and what she was all about as well as what she was determined to accomplish. She was strong and independent but it was obvious she used those traits and her life to do whatever she could to better the lives of others.

When Violet completed her presentation that day I was very inspired and I wanted to be just like her when I grew up!

Violet passed away on 2 August 1979. She was just 25 days short of her 91st birthday. Her memorial service was held on 15 August. At that time I was Founder Region Secretary and was honoured to be invited to sing the old and beloved hymn 'In the Garden' at her service. I wrote and included singing a special extra verse just for Violet.

That year the Soroptimist International of the Americas convention was held in Denver, Colorado. Violet was honoured there at a special service narrated by Catherine Burns who was then our Founder Region Governor.

Catherine's words were accompanied by a slide presentation of our Founder Region Redwood Grove which included a slide of the incredible tall Redwood tree named in Violet's memory. Once again I was invited to sing 'In the Garden' at the convention with my special verse for Violet. Truly Violet Richardson Ward touched many, many lives during her time on earth and I am so proud that mine was one of them.

It is now up to all of us to keep her spirit alive through our own participation and contributions through our Soroptimist membership.

Below are the words that I wrote for Violet to the hymn 'In the Garden':

Violet's there in the garden with Him, where her soul's at peace forever
Though we miss her so, with each thought we know, one day we'll be together
And we'll walk with her and we'll talk with her, and forever we'll be at home
In that heavenly place prepared for us, where our dear Violet's gone.

Susan Joyce (SI Dixon, California, USA)

Linda Calder *was born in the small country town of Warrnambool, Victoria, Australia. She left at the age of 12 with her family to travel to North Queensland, lived in Sydney for three years and is now based on the Redcliffe Peninsula, 30 minutes north of Brisbane. After completing Business College, Linda has worked as an Executive Assistant in various roles in Sydney and Brisbane and has also studied Event Management and Project Management. She is now looking forward to opening her own cafe by the sea. Linda joined the Club SI Pine Rivers (now SI Moreton North) in 2004, commencing as Club Secretary, then progressing to President and two years as the ESD delegate at Region. Linda enjoys walking with her Mum along the foreshore, a good cup of coffee and baking. Her partner Grant and Grant's two boys are heavily involved in the local soccer club and travel regularly to attend games.*

Women 4 Women

I began sponsoring women in 2008 after hearing about the Women 4 Women organisation at a Soroptimist meeting. I joined Soroptimist International soon afterwards and sponsored four women; three from Kosovo and one from Rwanda. The sponsorship money was used for education, transport to courses and medical treatment for their children. It enabled the women to receive training in an area of interest to them and then utilise these skills to obtain employment or go into business for themselves. Unfortunately, it is often quite difficult in war torn countries for these women to realise their dreams of employment and small business. The programme provided them with skills they didn't previously have and will afford them some hope for the future. To receive letters from these women who have lives where we could only imagine the pain, hardship and frustration of living in these countries, is truly inspiring. Their appreciation for something that amounts to a cup of coffee a day for us here in Australia was overwhelming. It took just a small contribution each month from us to make a significant difference for them.

Linda Calder (SI Moreton North, Australia)

Suman Lal *was born in Ra on the west coast of Fiji Island. She hails from a farming background and is a Bank Officer by profession. Suman is married to Dr Dhirendra Lal and they have two children. She has been a Soroptimist since early 1994, has been President of SI Fiji twice, National Rep of SI Fiji twice and Programme UN/Liaison Officer. Suman's hobbies include singing, art and fashion designing.*

Pink Womb

Way back in 1994, when Soroptimist International was re-chartered in the district of Sigatoka, Fiji, after a closure of ten years, I joined and am still a member. We took up a project on health screening for early detection and cure which included 'pap smear' tests as well. At the club meeting for this project, a member suggested that we should be screened first. It was arranged and we went through the process. My result was positive (infections found in the smear). I had to see a gynaecologist who carried out further tests on me. Eventually I had to have a hysterectomy in a timeframe of just a few months. This saved the spreading of infection to the possibility of me having cancer of the uterus. According to the doctors, if untreated, I would have lived for only another ten to 12 years. My surgery was in 1995!

Today, I am still healthy and going strong.

This is what being a Soroptimist has given me – my life!

Suman Lal (SI Sigatoka, Fiji)

Stella McKay-Moffat *was born in Folkestone, Kent, England, despite having a very Scottish name (husband number one was McKay; husband number two is Moffat). Stella has lived in the North West of England since 1973, mainly on the Wirral Peninsula with her husband David and their two dogs. Stella has a nursing background and was a midwife for 38 years practising as a university midwifery lecturer for the last 22 years before retiring in 2011. She is the author/editor of two textbooks for midwives and has spoken at national and international midwifery conferences. Stella has been a Soroptimist since 2000 and was President for two years of SI Wallasey, from 2011-13. She feels honoured to have been voted in to be President of the Region of Cheshire, North Wales and Wirral from 2014-15.*

Soroptimist Name Badge Baked

Soroptimist name badges don't bake well!

What's that on the oven bottom? The oven was heating, working its way to 190°C. I opened the oven door – I don't believe it, my Soroptimist name badge. A quick look revealed the named part of my badge on the oven floor and the magnetic strip firmly clinging to one of the oven racks. What on earth? Rapid removal, using oven gloves – it's hot.

Unnoticed, my magnetic name badge was on the kitchen table after removing it from my jacket. I had placed the (cold) shelf racks on the table whilst I re-arranged the shelf levels. Magnets doing what magnets do, the badge had attached itself to the bottom of the shelf which had then gone into the oven. Badge crinkled but just about usable; magnetic strip now complete with lined indentations. A unique badge now! Perhaps it's time to invest in a new one complete with new logo.

Motto(s):

Don't be slovenly, put badge away not on the kitchen table – I'm always careful with the President's chain so why not my badge?

The kitchen table should not be used as 'a dumping ground'.

Watch what I'm doing with the oven shelves.

Stella McKay-Moffat (SI Wallasey, England)

Julie Patel *has enjoyed being the Programme Action officer for SI Blackpool and District for the past two years. Although not 'sand grown' in Blackpool, she has lived in the Blackpool area for 25 years. As a little girl, it was one of the highlights for the family to pack a nice picnic, a bucket and spade, and to head to Blackpool for the day. A donkey ride and trip on the trams along the prom was usually incorporated. Julie works as a Clinical Psychologist in the NHS and still enjoys the attractions of bonnie Blackpool – the Vegas of the North!*

Vegas of the North

They say that Blackpool's like Vegas.
"Not quite", do I hear you say?
Well perhaps it's the Vegas of the North –
Things done in Lancastrian way

So what do we get up to,
In sunny Blackpool-on-sea,
What does our PA work entail?
Well – it's not just cakes and tea!

We have lots of long-term projects
Which have run for many a year.
We have two women's refuges
So that women can live without fear.

We 'man' Child Contact centres
Where families feel safe, and can meet,
We sell tea, coffee and biscuits
And we're often run off our feet.

We like to read the 'Lancashire' mag
For Blackpool folks with poor sight,
Putting together the 'Talking Books'
Which we do on a Wednesday night.

We've visited health centres and chemists
For the ovarian cancer campaign.
We've raised awareness and knowledge,
Given out leaflets again and again.

Now as you know in Blackpool
Things can be quite diverse.
We've jumped from 'opera' to toilets,
Let me tell you about it in verse.

We support the Purple Teardrop,
Which is very close to our hearts,
Signed petitions, and wear ribbons,
And we've even gone into the 'arts'.

We attended an opera in Manchester,
The premiere of Anya 17,
This described sex trafficking and abuse –
The problems that go unseen.

We wrote to the Chief Executive,
To ask for our Council's support,
"Can we put our posters in your toilets?"
Sent him the Purple Teardrop report.

We waited quite a long time,
Tried not to show our distress.
And eventually back came the answer,
The Council would like to say "Yes".

Well, now there are posters in toilets,
And leaflets in chemists' shops too.
And so we are thinking of next steps
Of what we would now like to do.

We have some plans to take forward,
And new innovations we seek,
And, just as it so happens,
It was Leeds UK PAC day last week.

 I look forward to the future
And although PA work's never done,
One thing about the Soroptimists
They do make it all great fun!

Julie Patel (SI Blackpool, England)

Lesley Rainford *was born in Aden, South Yemen – a forces baby. She was brought up in Wales and is a proud Welsh woman. She has lived and worked throughout the country as a Chartered Quantity Surveyor but settled down as a farmer's wife in 1994 when she married Andrew – a dairy farmer. She now works at a local Agricultural College as an Information and Guidance Advisor. She was Secretary to her Club SI Garstang from 2005-11, and Club President in 2011-12.*

Eating for Soroptimism

The President's guidance is all well and good
But it doesn't tell you just what it should
Now *you* are President – learn to eat
Forget intolerances to sweet or wheat
Get in the car once a month
And travel afar to enjoy a lunch
Evening meals and afternoon teas
You're always able to choose what you please
Don't kid yourself that you can resist
To turn down a cake would get you dismissed
So before you agree to that nomination
Ensure that your mind has domination

Don't end up like me
Gaining a stone or three!

Lesley Rainford (SI Garstang, England)

A Very Brief Glimpse

She came back into the house and out of the November wind with a sense of a job well done. Cheeks reddened and so cold that the tears that fell from her eyes felt as if they might freeze. She could still taste the morning, the promise of snow to come, the salty tang of the Irish Sea; could feel the crisp seaweed under foot as she had walked the dogs.

Hanging up her jacket she smiled at the jumble of poo bags and dog treats that fell out of her pockets as she missed the peg in the pantry first time around. "I am turning into my mother", she thought. The house smelled of the scones she had baked before she went out – fat, oversized scones begging to be sliced open and filled with butter and the damson jam that her friend Olive had made.

Filling the kettle she popped it onto the range and got to work on the sandwiches – tasty, savoury sandwiches with satisfying fillings suitable for a winter's day. The kettle started to sing and the small bird whistle vibrated and tweeted with the steam that poured through its mouth.

Putting the dogs into the garden room, treats in a bowl, she hugged them both but refused to let them back into the sitting room. Beautiful dogs but totally untrustworthy around food. She laid the soft white cloth that had belonged to her grandmother onto the sideboard. Her grandmother had run her home and garden with a firm hand but always had time for her granddaughters. She had left bits of her china and linen to each of them when she died. Treated with care they evoked a sense of continuity and today they glowed gently in the firelight, her china and linen now.

That morning she had given everything a thorough clean and the house smelled of furniture polish and lavender. She checked the towels, loo rolls and soap in the bathroom and cloakroom, no children at home to throw the towels down carelessly and leave the soap in the basin.

Their happy, seemingly unnoticed chaos shared now with other younger people with more energy, all of them happy and content. She loved her children but also loved the space in the house, the sense of just the two of them again and the promise of weekends away exploring small towns and walking the dogs on unknown beaches and hillsides.

A car door slammed outside and then another, the sound of laughing voices, women calling greetings and the rat-a-tat-tat of the dolphin knocker. The voices came closer into the hall.

"BOOTS OFF", she yelled and the door opened onto a jumble of women of all sizes carrying folders and small plastic boxes, the contents of which promised to add to the sandwiches and scones in an agreeable way. No diets today!

When everyone was seated and welcomed, the list for teas and coffees taken through into the kitchen and the cups warming alongside the tea and coffee pots ("caffeine free for three" she mumbled to herself). The plates and napkins handed out; she glanced around the group, women of different sizes, different ages, some still involved with jobs that ask more of them each year, some retired involved in voluntary work and Edyth, looking forward to her 90th birthday – frail but still engaged with the other women, ready with a word of encouragement and friendship.

She looked at her notes and announced, "Welcome to our second Programme Action Meeting, any apologies?"

Brenda Lynton-Escreet (SI Morecambe and Heysham, England)

You May Never Know What You Leave Behind
A Valuable Lesson Learned

My Soroptimist club had planned to spread some warm Valentine's Day cheer
by visiting a local assisted living centre in February of that year
We'd bring bright helium balloons and old fashioned Valentine cards too
Hand delivering them to the elderly residents there that none of us knew

The plan was to tie the balloons to wheelchairs and also to each occupied bed
We'd walk down halls into each room and personally deliver the cards that said
That each of them were remembered and cared for on this special heart day
We'd spend some time chatting and visiting as we went on down the long
hallway

We also brought hearts that were stickers that on their hands we'd place
Making our visit personal… touching… making contact face to face
It warmed our hearts to do this, and when it was time for us to go
The rooms looked so bright and colourful, the residents lively and aglow

A week later as I sat in my hairdresser's chair, I related our visit to her
And how very good we all felt after visiting the residents there
She said, "So that was your club? I heard all about your visit that day
My little client Helga told me about it…this is what she had to say"

"She visits her husband there every day though he doesn't respond and just
stares
She talks to him, combs his hair and, touching his hand, saw the heart sticker
there
He was holding a Valentine card and tied to his wheelchair was a balloon in
flight
She said the place seemed so warm and cheery, with everyone happy and light"

"She made her usual visit, chatted away though he didn't respond or react
When she stood up to go, he looked up…his eyes meeting hers making direct
contact
And slowly tearing his Valentine in two, he placed one half in the palm of her
hand

Though not audibly spoken, 'twas a loving gesture and so easy to understand"

I would never have known about the magical moment that happened on that
day
When a gift of simple hands on service was extended in a loving and caring
way
I've shared this story many times when I've spoken at meetings over the years
bringing goose bumps when each time I look out and see I'm not the only one
in tears

I always close by sharing what this life changing story has come to mean to me
to encourage my audience to keep giving and doing for others in their
community
The valuable lesson I learned that day is you may never know what you leave
behind
But be assured something good will always come from being generous, caring
and kind.

Susan Joyce (SI Dixon, California, USA)

Anne Nugent *was born in Dublin, Ireland in the early 1900s and has lived there all of her life. Anne worked as an accountant with the Royal Insurance Group until her retirement. Since then Anne has been a highly valued and dedicated member of the Soroptimist International Club of Dublin for over 40 years. She is a Past President and was also Club Secretary for six years. Anne has attended many International and Federation conferences throughout the world and wrote 'The Joy of Being a Soroptimist' in 1993.*

Attracta

Many years ago the Hon. Beatrice Grosvenor, daughter of the then Duke of Leinster, married and, living in Killarney, (she retained her maiden name) was National President of Southern Ireland. At her National Conference members came from far and wide, especially from the United States of America. Those members were all staying in the Hibernian Hotel, Dawson Street in Dublin. My club, SI Dublin, was consequently very involved in offering friendship and hospitality to our visitors – in a true, warm Irish style! On the day of their departure a committee member was at hand to give them any help needed. She organised taxis for them and said that Attracta would take their luggage to the airport. One of the Soroptimist's husbands looked amazed and said,

"Gee, this is a great country! They even have a tractor to take our luggage to the airport!"

Attracta, a member of SI Dublin, often used to tell this story!

Anne Nugent (SI Dublin, Republic of Ireland)

Thelma de Leeuw *is a Londoner who has now spent more than half her life working in Yorkshire. Trained as a musician, she later moved from music education lecturing to College Management and Student Advice roles. Exposed to Soroptimist influence since the age of ten, Thelma joined SI Bingley in 1966 and experienced life as Club and Region Secretary and President, Federation President, International President 1989-91 and coordinator of Project Five-O. These responsibilities, often in warmer climes, gave her a taste for travelling with a purpose. With her preference being for cooler temperatures, she has more recently explored parts of Scandinavia, Greenland, Arctic Canada and Antarctica. Her next voyage is a circumnavigation of Newfoundland. Her other passion is volunteer service to Bradford Cathedral.*

Senior Status!

At work, on my 60th birthday, my admin colleagues presented me with an A1-sized copy of the application form for what in my city was known then as an Elderly Person's Bus Pass. Some weeks later, proud possessor of an as yet unused Pass, I arrived at the ticket window of a London Underground station and decided to see what the Pass could do. "What do I get for having this?" was my innocent question. With the sweetest smile in the world the elderly person on the other side of the glass replied, as he printed out a full-fare ticket, "Madam, I regret – nothing but my respect and admiration". Quite made my day!

And this reminded me of an earlier occasion, when I was Federation President arriving to charter a club on the other side of the world, accompanied by two medical doctor members from the UK. The capital's international airport seemed to be the regular place for people-watching on a Saturday night out. Ushered through the arrival formalities we arrived at the final security check before being let loose on the city and our individual arrivals were announced at full volume: Doctor Mrs Jean – loud applause – Jean was well-known in the country already. Doctor Mrs Kate – respectful applause – like myself Kate was a first-time visitor but with a professional interest in specialist ophthalmic work at the city hospitals. Long Pause. Some puzzlement. President…Miss Thelma… another pause… Miss? More respectful applause. But the official continued –

"Miss…is it true?" I agreed it was. Again, a very sweet smile. "What a pity!"

Loud applause…

Thelma de Leeuw (SI Bingley, England)

Sisterhood of Women

Women of the world, girls of the planet,
We are all sisters.
Traumas and joys that happen to one,
Happen to us all.
Issues and rights, oppression and empowerment
Are part of woman's challenge for equality, for dignity,
For we are bonded in the female spirit.
We reach out to learn, to understand each other.
Local to global, rural and urban, near to far, hugs and tears,
Now is our time!

Lois Herman (SI Greater Minneapolis, Minnesota, USA)

JUST TALES

Su Rennison *was born in Halifax, Yorkshire, England. She was brought up in Worcestershire but has lived in Kent for most of her working life. Su has had two careers. The first as a tutor/librarian working in Higher Education Colleges, and the second as the Christian Stewardship Adviser for the Church of England Diocese of Canterbury. A Soroptimist since her early 30s, Su has been President of SI Canterbury twice, 1979-80 and 1987-88. In 2012, Su was made an Honorary Member of the club. Su is married to John. They both enjoy reading, walking and the theatre. As amateur musicians playing 'cello and viola they have been described as 'the back legs of a String Quartet!'*

Lest We Forget

We were a mixed group waiting on the station that Friday morning. It included a 12 year old with his father – refugees from Romania now living in Germany, a gaggle of teenagers agog with excitement, several ladies of indeterminate age with no English and our friends Fritz and Inge. The link between us was music. We were part of two amateur orchestras coming together for a concert the following evening. For their first visit to the UK a trip to London was a must.

So we joined our friends, sneaking off for the day disguised as tourists. Arriving at Victoria Station the teenagers melted into the crowds as if they had evaporated into thin air; not to be seen again until we boarded the train home. So much for Fritz's role as parental guardian.

A much depleted group looked expectantly at John and me. "We do not want to go inside" said Fritz, "Just give us a feel of London and show us the main sights". So, our disguise in tatters we became very very pale 'Blue Badge Guides' instead. Neither of us knew London that well. We could tread a deep furrow to Kings College or Deans Yard Westminster for meetings but that was hardly the agenda for today. Naturally we had not brought a map.

However with stiff upper lips we looked confident, avoided looking at each other and strode out of the station. We strolled smartly up Buckingham Palace Road. As we reached the Palace Gates they were just beginning to change the Guard. It was not the short procedure relieving one spell of duty for another but a complete change of Regiment. Military bands, ceremonial drill, shouted orders and loads of presentation of arms etc. Our party took it all for granted, captured a few shots on camera and assumed that this took place every 20 minutes or so. We did not say that it only took place once every two months, nor that our timing was purely accidental.

Instead we launched across Victoria Square into Bird Cage Walk through St James Park and down to Westminster Abbey. After a quick glance through the West Door it was over London Bridge and along the Embankment to survey the glory of the Houses of Parliament and Big Ben. Walking by the Thames taking in the city's sky scrapers surrounding St Paul's Cathedral, I marvelled at how beautiful London is when you have time to stare. It is too easy to take for granted its history and culture. The whole atmosphere seems to stand witness to our vibrant democratic way of life.

We dived into the bustle and noise of Covent Garden and as we gathered together to decide where to lunch we discovered we were one lady short. Unable to do a thing about her, we carried on. From time to time John would casually glance over Fritz's shoulder to read *his* map and in this way we meandered through theatre land and finally into Oxford Street. Here our feet gave out and we plunged into Oxford Circus tube station. It was the rush hour and Inge, desperate to buy us our tickets, had her purse snatched by a very pretty, well-heeled but light fingered office worker. Gone in a flash were her identity card, health card and money.

Back at Victoria Station we were reunited with our teenagers and the lost lady. She had popped into a shop without telling anyone and when she emerged we were out of sight. With no English, she had stopped everyone who passed her until she found a German speaker. They directed her back to Victoria Station, where she had spent the whole of the day. Feeling partly to blame we retreated into oblivion and slept most of the journey home.

Later that night we assessed our gains and losses. "Not the most successful day out" commented John. Then we remembered the moment of awe and humility. Our Romanian lawyer, who had fled his own country, who could no longer practice his profession in Germany, who played Fritz's second best violin; a man of peace, gentleness and integrity, had taken both our hands in his and with tears in his eyes thanked us. "Today" he said "I have never felt so free".

Susan Rennison (SI Canterbury, England)

Old Wives Tales have been handed down from generation to generation. Different countries and different areas within them often have their own special folklore. Here are a few such 'tales' from Lancashire, but they also include 'tales' from the Black Country and Worcestershire - in the heart of England.

Some Old-Fashioned Home Remedies

Grandma Phillips lived in Wordsley, Kingswinford, in England's Black Country and my Grandma Harper lived in Kidderminster, Worcestershire. They both told me many old-fashioned home remedies. In turn, I am passing them on to you. I wonder if you recognise any of them and in how many more counties – even countries – can they be found?

Comfrey (known as Knitbone) helps sprains and broken bones.

Brimstone and treacle, mixed together, purifies the blood.

Goose grease is beneficial for colds and sore throats, especially if it is rubbed on the chest and covered in brown paper. I can still smell the grease – not a pleasant memory, but it did seem to work!

Balm tea calms the nervous system.

Raspberry leaves, boiled to drink, helps in childbirth.

Oatmeal poultices help cure acne and boils. Again, they did work. I can remember the tin they were made in, boiling away in a saucepan on the black leaded kitchen grate.

Linseed oil, with some onion, clears a congested chest.

A soap and sugar poultice can remove a splinter from a finger.

The drink Vimto was first mixed as 'Vimtonic' by Mr John Noel Nichols of Manchester in 1908. It is a unique combination of fruit juices, spices, herbs and nuts and became an immediate success. It is still enjoyed today. It is one of my granddaughter's favourite drinks!

How many of these did you recognise or remember from your own childhood?

Eileen Clarke (SI Leyland, England)

Patricia Maki (Pat) *was born in San Diego, California, USA. When she was three her family moved to Eagle Rock, a suburb of Los Angeles, where she grew up. Pat married Leo and had three daughters. Leo's work moved the family to Oxnard, California in 1964, where they still reside. While her daughters were in college she too finished her education to become a certified public accountant. She established her own practice and, after 20 years, sold it to become more active with her grandchildren, the community and in Soroptimist International of Oxnard. Pat has been an active Soroptimist for 26 years. She and her husband travelled extensively until he fell victim to dementia.*

Intruder

I am retired and busy. I, with help, caregive my husband and am active in Soroptimist International and other Boards. Every morning, after the mayhem of getting my husband on the bus for daycare, and after the dog takes me for a walk, I enjoy a quiet cup of tea and the newspaper.

One morning my absent neighbour's burglar alarm suddenly went off. It is an amazingly loud and irritating sound…*woOowOoO.* I have a key to their house and the code for their alarm…so I grabbed the key and with a barking dog, raced over. *WoHoWoOo.* Whoops…wrong key! *WOoHoO* bark…BARK, bark! We race home and back with the right key, punch in the number and enter the house. *WOOhooO.* Whoops…wrong number! *WoHoOo…*BARK, bark, bark! We race home and check the number, race back…*wHoOoho…*yip, yip, YIP, punch in the right number and enter the house again. Alarm silences. Dog stops barking…Quiet…Then the police show up, dog starts barking, police check house, talk, talk, bark, bark and then……Quiet!

Back to the tea and paper.

That night my neighbours gave me a chicken for dinner. The intruder?

Such is life!

Patricia Maki (SI Oxnard, California, USA)

Japanese Poetry Party 'Kyokusui no Utage'

In Japan, there was once a period in our history called 'Heian' (794 to 1185). It was considered to be when the Japanese Imperial Court was as its peak and was particularly noted for its poetry and literature.

During this time, a poetry party called 'Kyokusui no Utage' was held at the Imperial Court in Kyoto City.

Participants dressed in their elegant court robes and sat along the banks of the winding stream in a garden of the Court. Cups of rice wine, 'Sake', were floated down the stream and the participants had to improvise a 31-syllable Japanese poem before the cup reached each participant's position!

Participants enjoyed the poetry but they also enjoyed drinking Sake!

This party is still held at several shrines today so that the Japanese of this century can appreciate and inherit the valuable culture of this special period in our history.

Kuniko Osawa (SI Tokyo Azuma, Japan)

The Phone Call

I really had to get rid of some of my hoarded paperwork – drawers stuffed with junk mail, cards, notices of functions that had long since taken place and goodness knows what else! This job of de-cluttering was on the agenda for a long time but I had a free morning and decided to get started on with this unwelcome task.

Early morning, good breakfast and down to business! I was going to do the job drawer by drawer but got rather enthusiastic and tipped the contents of the three drawers on to the floor. Big mistake! I made three piles – rubbish, papers for shredding and hopefully a small pile that was to be examined and re-sorted!

Got stuck in – tuned to RTE Radio 1 – worked energetically through John Murray, slowed down a bit during Pat Kenny and was just halfway through Ronan Collins when the phone rang. It was a friend, who had a mutual acquaintance visiting and she said they would pop over after lunch for a chat. My friend knew I was free all day so I could not plead a prior engagement! What was I going to do?

I almost panicked. Thank God I had a decent bottle of wine which I had put to chill in the fridge. I polished three good glasses, set out nuts and crisps in bowls and located some posh napkins.

But what was I going to do with the chaos? First, I put the three piles into the bedroom. Then, the remaining paper had to be shoved back willy-nilly into the three drawers. Sorting of this would be a job for another day!

The floor had to be vacuumed. That lovely Jasmine floral room spray, a Christmas present, got a good blast. The heat was turned on full and the windows opened for half an hour. The place began to look respectable. I made a quick clothes change and slapped on some make-up. Then…I took three deep breaths and emerged – the perfect hostess waiting to entertain my guests!

We had a wonderful afternoon catching up and gossiping as only friends can! De-cluttering…well, perhaps another day?

'The best laid schemes of mice and men . . . . !'

Monica Barry (SI Sligo, Republic of Ireland)

Candlesticks

She arrived for dinner on Friday night.

The candles were lit, but not in the usual Russian silver candlesticks. They burned in cheap metal holders.

The beautiful silver bowl had also disappeared as well as the gorgeous vase left by her deceased grandmother.

"Where has all the silver gone?" her daughter wailed.

"I sold it all plus other heirlooms" replied her mother.

"You took my car and keys and said I was no longer capable of driving. I took a driving test, passed and bought myself a new car."

She pointed at the open window, "Look, a Mercedes Benz."

Hannah Lurie (SI Durban, South Africa)

This is a true story – but the car was not a Mercedes!

Sue Pritt *was born in Birmingham, England, moved to London in 1966 and retired to the Kent coast 40 years later. Her London Local Government career culminated as Assistant Director of Leisure Services explaining her scant knowledge of burials, trees, landscaping, grounds maintenance and golf courses. A Soroptimist since her mid 30s, Sue is a member of SI Canterbury, but is also attached to SI Cape of Good Hope for the five months annually she lives in South Africa. She has been Club President of SI Richmond, Surrey and SI Kingston upon Thames and Regional President and Regional Treasurer of SI Southern England.*

A Bird in the Hand…Or the Cage

We're going away, they said, can you look after Napoleon for us? The name should have been warning enough. After all we'd looked after Simon every Christmas for a while, an engaging guy with a good vocabulary, so what problem could Napoleon pose?

I should explain, Simon and Napoleon are parrots. Simon was a joy to have and during his first stay kept our kitten on his toes by mewing, barking or shouting "Hello" at him!

Napoleon duly arrived, along with his owners, concerned we'd look after him just as he was at home. His cage duly deposited on the table assigned for it, the prospect of looking after him nose-dived. He only drank bottled water, only ate brown toast, only liked butter on that, and it had to be cut up into fingers. Did they realise this was a favour, not a boarding facility? Oh, they said as they left, don't forget to stick the piece of wood into the space left when you take out his water.

They finally went and Napoleon celebrated by helicoptering – revving up his wings – very impressive except he didn't takeoff, every last bird seed did, and flew around the room.

Next day I set about the feeding routine, as I was removing the water container – don't forget it's bottled water, not tap, the phone rang. So naturally I went to answer it and called my husband to take the call. Coming down the stairs from doing this, I could not believe my eyes, passing me going down the hall was... Napoleon. Oh heavens, I'd forgotten the wood – this bird is an escape artist.

Parrot catching is not a skill I've ever needed to possess. Simon never escaped. He was a well-trained bird. Some fast thinking was required; I had to stop Napoleon from reaching the cat flap – easy to open with a gentle shove – or indeed reaching the cats. Not sure who would have come off worst, but I just knew a dead (late?) parrot was not an option. Neither was a mauled cat. I needed something to save my hands from his claws. Bingo! Oven gloves! So, racing past him, I grabbed them and advanced. One sight of the gloves and he became a whirling, squawking monster. Why didn't they tell me he hates having his claws cut and the only way to catch him? Yes, you guessed, with oven gloves!

Retiring, slightly dazed, to the kitchen there seemed only one answer – his cage. I retrieved that from its base, cornered him only feet from the cat flap, and triumphantly plonked it on top of him. Elation lasted seconds; here I was with him trapped, but on our carpet. The cats were by now patrolling round the cage, and parrots are no respecters of toileting facilities. So, off again to get the base of the cage. As a result of the phone call, my husband had already gone out, so the conundrum – how to get the cage onto the base without Napoleon taking flight? Thank goodness for that toast – he hardly noticed being elevated and returned to his allotted spot.

Me – I needed a strong cup of coffee, and an even stronger resolve. So, the following year when the call came it was not hard to say we wouldn't be around. My parrot minding days were at an end. There is a sting in the tail – a red tail; Simon is an African Grey, now living in Branscombe, Devon. His owner, ten years older than me, always said she'd leave him to me in her will. We've moved a couple of times since we last saw her.

Will her Executors ever find me – who knows?

Sue Pritt (SI Canterbury, England)

Audrey Butterworth *has loved singing all her life. It was at her primary school in Bury, Lancashire, England, that her love of sacred music was fostered and she joined her church choir when she was 13 years old. Audrey wanted to be a soprano but was devastated when her voice developed into contralto! She sang solo contralto in all the major oratorios, including 'The Messiah' and 'Elijah'. Audrey married another musician, Harry, and became a cabaret performer after her three children were born. In spite of having problems with asthma she managed to continue with her singing career and eventually went into Old Time Music Hall on tour, performing in theatres all over the country. She also sang in Jacobean banquets and, with her husband, formed a group, 'The Stuart Singers', who performed a variety of themed music evenings at Hoghton Towers near Preston. In between concerts Audrey also worked on a number of television series, including 'Hallelujah', with Thora Hird and 'Sister Dora' with Dorothy Tutin. Audrey was introduced to Soroptimism through her singing teacher Edith Norcross, by inviting her to sing at functions for SI Bolton. Audrey loves being a Soroptimist! She joined Bury club in 1987 and was President in 1996-97 and again in 2000-01. Later, because of family commitments, she transferred to SI Bootle and was President in 2005-06.*

A Ghostly Encounter

It was a grey Yorkshire morning. The mist was swirling through the branches of trees – pointing like arthritic witches' fingers and the constant drizzle was relentless. It was not a morning to be lost… but I was! My smart, brand new bright red Toledo the only splash of colour in an otherwise colourless world.

I had parked by the side of the road and walked a little way to see if I could find a shop or even a signpost: to no avail. It wasn't an isolated place though and there seemed to be plenty of passing traffic – commuters on their early morning drive to work.

I began to be worried about being late. The producer would not be keen to cast me again if he thought that I was unreliable. It was only a small part, but it had been a film that I had really enjoyed making – and it had given me the amazing opportunity of working with Dorothy Tutin.

We had been filming 'Sister Dora', a mini-series for Yorkshire Television. I am a professional actress and singer, and I was playing the part of a nurse. It was an inspiring story, based on the real-life character of Dorothy Pattison. Her father forbade her to marry the man she loved and she became an Anglican nun. Sister Dora's nursing skills and personal heroism had saved many lives on a number of occasions – including during the disaster at Pelsall Colliery in 1872. The make-up for this scene was particularly effective… and quite horrifying!

We thought that we had actually finished all the filming, but I was contacted to do one more re-take – the death scene. My role was to care for the ailing Sister Dora at the end of her life. Transport was usually provided but on this occasion I was asked if I would drive myself. "It won't be a problem," they said, "Just follow the driver in front of you. The cottage we are using is just past the crematorium, towards Guisely. You will be fine!"

At that hour of the morning, in the swirling grey mist, however, I was not fine! The driver I was supposed to tail lost me at a set of traffic lights. Instead of waiting for me, he had just gone on!

I knew, by then, that I was very late… and also very wet! To save time – ironically as it turned out – I had already changed into my costume before leaving home. I wore a long grey dress, a grey cap and a starched white 'pinnie' – all set off with the grey cape worn by a nurse during the latter half of the nineteenth century. I had a pinched, grey face without any make-up. A damp, grey nurse on a damp grey kerbside!

I noticed that people were giving me strange looks as they drove past. Some sped on, putting their foot on the accelerator. One woman even drove on, then reversed, to get a closer look at me! "How rude", I thought. They might, at least, have stopped and asked if they could help. Wasn't it obvious that I was lost?

At last, I finally managed to flag down a passer-by. It was raining quite hard by then – and the mist had really settled around me. "Could you tell me the way to the crematorium?" I asked. Not waiting to reply, he also turned a shade of grey…and drove off without a word!

I walked back to my car, wet and disgruntled. It was then that I saw the signpost, half-hidden by foliage. After all that, I was not far from my destination!

It was at that moment that I realised why my presence had prompted so many strange looks…and my destination caused sheer panic. I was dressed in full costume…from a long-distant age!

I was still laughing when I eventually arrived at the location. It was no longer a grey Yorkshire morning!

Audrey Butterworth (SI Bootle, England)

Bonaventure

We waited for the bus on the steep Via Sistina in Rome.

Walking towards us were seven or eight monks in brown cassocks. I informed my husband excitedly that these were Dominican monks. I recognised their cassocks as I had just read about them, their lifestyle, growing all their produce and being famous for inventing Dom Benedictine, the brilliant liqueur. They drew abreast of us and I heard, "Hannah!" I jumped!

"Hinwood!" I shrilled. I recognised the prefect from my old high school. We embraced with laughter as my husband's mouth fell open in shock.

The other monks walked on.

Hannah Lurie (SI Durban, South Africa)

This is a true story. I was at High School with Edward Hinwood who became Father Bonaventure Hinwood!

Anzac Day at Deception Bay

Dawn hasn't arrived yet as I stand on the beachfront at Deception Bay awaiting the sunrise. A full moon still lingers in the night sky. The tide is out and there is no wind. The only sound is the dull din of preparations for the early morning service.

This has always been my favourite time to remember the ANZACS. To remind myself of others that have come after them who lost their lives in battle and those that came home to tell their stories (and those that could not).

My heart goes out to the families who have only memories and photographs as a reminder of lost loved ones who made the ultimate sacrifice defending our freedom. I am reminded of the innocent lives that have been lost and are still being lost especially the women and children who are often considered collateral damage in war or perhaps not even considered at all?

As the tide silently creeps into shore and laps around my ankles, it is cold but somehow comforting. I gaze out at the formation of the clouds on the horizon – they depict the signs of battle. Is it possible that this is a reflection of the tumult that occurred so many years ago on the sands of a distant cove? Is it their ANZAC spirit I can feel or is it just my imagination?

The drums and the bagpipes are warming up – a signal that the dawn service is about to begin. Hundreds of young people and families are lining up to commemorate the fallen and watch the veterans march. I don't need to linger for the speeches that will follow – I've been to many before. I pay my respects to those young brave souls as I watch the sun rise.

Throughout the day and at the going down of the sun, I will remember them and each and every other day too. May we all spend a quiet moment thinking about those that still live and struggle to survive in conflict zones around the world and those that work at many levels to protect them!

May Global Peace be our Uniting Purpose – Lest We Forget.

I know I shall not forget their stories.

(*Chris Knight, SI Moreton North, Australia*)

Mankind has always been fascinated by the untold tales hidden in the sky. By day, cloud formations tell their own tales of castles, dragons and dreams… But at night, the sky tells its own tales which are beyond our imagination. Legends from the Ancient World personified the sun and the moon. Gazing at them takes us to the edge of wonder.

Moon Songs

the morning moon
is a cashew nut
crooning a perfumed tune
in time –
so fal so fal, lal la

at noon the moon's
a lemon slice
with a lemonade song
on her lips –
la fa ha ha, la laa

the midnight moon
is dark as a plum
and hums a nocturne
bitter sweet –
so la la la can ta
as
she thinks of her waxing
and waning,
immutable waxing
and waning.

Hilary Semple (SI Johannesburg, South Africa)

Index by Author

Authors

As featured on the rear cover *(from left to right)*

Top row: Val Christoffersen, Eileen Clarke, Mary Clarke, Sheilah Downs, Jacque Emery, Brenda Lynton-Escreet, Pat Fergusson.

Second row: Nisha Ghosh, Ann Greenfield, Erene Grieve, Pansy Griffith, Clare Harding, Lois Herman, Susan Joyce.

Third row: Promila Khandelwal, Chris Knight, Suman Lal, Joan Lees, Thelma de Leeuw, Hannah Lurie, Patricia Maki.

Fourth row: Mary McCormick, Stella McKay-Moffat, Barbara Milburn, Heather Nestel, Margaret Sharon Olscamp, Anne Nugent, Julie Patel.

Fifth row: Sue Pritt, Lesley Rainford, Rema Ramchandran, Ann Reeves, Su Rennison, Marja Reunis de Rechter, Carol Salter.

Sixth row: Hilary Semple, Kate Sergeant, Lexi Smart, Jo Spencer, Ann Truscott, Audrey Butterworth, Linda Calder.

Bottom row: Monica Barry, Anita Belagodu, Lieske Bester, Marie Blacktop, Hannah Mili Boteiova.